SECRETS OF THE
CASTLETON
MANOR LIBRARY™

From Fable to Grave

Marlene Chase

Annie's®
AnniesFiction.com

Books in the Secrets of the Castleton Manor Library series

Library of Congress-in-Publication Data
From Fable to Grave / by Marlene Chase
p. cm.
I. Title
                    2018955140

AnniesFiction.com
(800) 282-6643
Secrets of the Castleton Manor Library™
Series Creator: Shari Lohner
Series Editor: Lorie Jones
Cover Illustrator: Jesse Reisch

10 11 12 13 14 | Printed in South Korea | 9 8 7 6 5 4

1

Faith Newberry stooped to touch the petals of a daffodil blooming near the front door of her cottage. The sprightly flower held its buttery cup to the April sky. No wonder the poet William Wordsworth could dance with the flowers at the very thought of them.

"Careful, Rumpy," she cautioned as the cat leaped off the step into the flowers, whiskers twitching.

The black-and-white cat gave his stub of a tail a brief wiggle—the only indication that he had heard—and scampered off.

Of course, he might have been responding with disdain to her use of the undignified moniker Rumpy instead of his perfectly appropriate name, which was Watson. Clever and curious, the tuxedo cat had a knack for solving mysteries that the great Sherlock Holmes would have applauded.

Faith watched Watson zigzag in the general direction of Castleton Manor, where he was as much at home as in his owner's cottage. There he would spend part of his day among the towering shelves of books, exploring the tantalizing nooks and crannies of the grand library.

It had been a singular delight to learn that Watson and other pets were welcome at the manor, invited to accompany their owners to retreats.

"Behave yourself," she called after her cat, laughing.

But Faith wasn't really worried that Watson would find some mischief to get into. Not today. It was a glorious morning, chilly but alive with the scents and sounds of spring in Massachusetts. Winter had been long and cold, and despite the beauty of Cape Cod, she yearned for warming breezes and the resurrection of nature after its extended sleep.

She made her way to the French Renaissance mansion that loomed tall in the azure sky, magnificent turrets and balconies shimmering in the light. The Jaxon family had turned the luxurious manor into a booklovers' haven and welcomed guests into its spectacular halls, parlors, and suites. Guests could revel in its château-style beauty, wander the splendid halls, and gaze out on breathtaking views of the ocean.

Sometimes Faith couldn't quite believe her good fortune to work at the manor, where she'd been hired as the librarian and given a lovely, renovated cottage on its mammoth grounds. She was a long way from Boston and the hectic pace of the city. When she'd come to Lighthouse Bay, she had felt at home almost from the beginning.

Her roots were here, and she had found herself delving more and more deeply into them and growing a life rich with friendship and purpose. She missed her parents, but it helped that her favorite aunt was only a short distance away. A longtime resident of Lighthouse Bay, Eileen Piper was the head librarian at the privately funded Candle House Library and the leader of the Candle House Book Club. Faith and her aunt shared a love of literature and enjoyed friendship with the other members of the book club. Faith didn't take any of this for granted.

She glanced at her watch. *No more dawdling among the daffodils. And pass on by those impressive magnolia trees opening in the morning sunshine. Work awaits.*

Guests were arriving at the manor for the nineteenth-century American literature retreat, featuring the works of Mark Twain.

In 1935, Ernest Hemingway said, "All modern American literature comes from one book by Mark Twain called *Huckleberry Finn*." His comment referenced the colloquial language of Twain's masterpiece, as for perhaps the first time in America, the vivid, raw, not-so-respectable voice of the common folk was used to create great literature.

The retreat would also consider other writings of the period and genre. And the lovely seacoast town of Lighthouse Bay, with its maritime features and delightful shops, would provide a fitting ambience for the literary event.

Faith had been looking forward to the retreat. She'd brushed up on nineteenth-century American authors—Twain in particular—since she knew Marlene Russell, the manor's assistant manager, had arranged for a performance by an impressionist of the famous author. Marlene had planned other events as well, including a fashion show and various seminars highlighting the works of renowned authors of the period.

Faith could feel her enthusiasm rising as she anticipated meeting guests who came from many parts of the country and walks of life. Each would share a common interest in authors such as Bret Harte, Edith Wharton, Herman Melville, Harriet Beecher Stowe, and a host of others. In addition, it was always exciting to meet the visiting pets who were catered to with expert care.

She could no longer see Watson, who could fly on his four white paws like the wind when he wanted to.

As Faith entered the manor and passed through the Great Hall Gallery, she glanced at the loggia that provided a view of the ocean glittering in the sun. In the distance, the ancient lighthouse watched over the bay with solemnity and grace. She hurried on. Guests might be needing her assistance.

Marlene was waiting with a guest in the hall outside the library. The assistant manager glanced up at Faith from the clipboard she was studying, her pale-green eyes mildly accusatory. She wore a tailored olive pantsuit with a striped scarf that perfectly coordinated with her outfit, and her blonde hair was styled in a no-nonsense bun at the nape of her neck. Always the consummate professional, Marlene meticulously organized every detail of the manor's retreats, and she expected her staff to effectively carry out her plans.

"Good morning," Faith said cheerily as she approached.

"Ah, here she is now," Marlene said crisply.

Marlene's companion appraised Faith through eyes magnified by enormous thick-rimmed glasses. The woman was fortyish with dark hair that fell stylishly over the left side of her face. She was shorter than Marlene, but her posture was equally commanding. She wore a navy-blue suit with a crimson necktie. Faith thought the tie resembled one her father might have worn as a young man.

"Edna Grimmell, I'd like you to meet our librarian, Faith Newberry," Marlene said, then turned to Faith. "Miss Grimmell is Declan Ames's assistant and publicist."

Faith recalled that Declan Ames was the Mark Twain impressionist. Who could forget a name like Declan? Perhaps it was Irish or Australian. Faith held out her hand to Edna. "I'm glad to meet you. We're all looking forward to Mr. Ames's performance."

Edna's grasp was firm and cool. "Thank you," she said with a voice equally cool.

"You can be confident that Miss Newberry will help you with research or whatever Mr. Ames might need in the library," Marlene continued, her tone businesslike.

Edna's lips curved into enough of a smile to render her younger than Faith had first thought. "Then I shall rely on you," she said with an imperious air. "Mr. Ames is very particular in his tastes. He will be eager to see what Twain materials are available in the library."

"I'd be happy to give you a short tour," Faith said, unlocking the door and holding it open for Edna. "Please come inside."

As Edna entered the library, she gazed around the room. She didn't make any remarks about the luxurious interior.

Faith and Marlene followed her inside.

"Have you heard anything from Brooke this morning?" Marlene asked Faith. "I know she's been off for a couple days, but I expected to find her in the kitchen by now. Miss Grimmell needs to discuss Mr. Ames's dietary restrictions with her."

Faith frowned. It wasn't like Brooke to be late, especially when a new batch of guests was expected. "I'm sure she'll be here soon," she said protectively.

Brooke Milner was one of Faith's first friends at the manor. The head chef had helped her navigate the huge estate as a newbie, and she was a member of the Candle House Book Club.

"Mr. Ames is fastidious about his health, especially his diet," Edna said. "He had a heart attack last year, so his food must be free of gluten and salt, and sugar is to be limited in preparing his meals."

Faith stifled a sigh. Declan sounded like a high-maintenance guest, and Edna was acting more like his mother than an assistant or a publicist.

"Brooke Milner, our head chef, will gladly accommodate all of his needs," Marlene assured Edna. "I'm sure you'll be able to speak with her soon."

"I certainly hope so," Edna said. "We're down to the last minute, and I have a great deal to discuss with the chef."

"And you'll find various research materials and other books right here." Faith ushered Edna deeper into the library, indicating the impressive floor-to-ceiling shelves of books. Then she pointed to the locked glass cases. "The first editions are over there—"

A bloodcurdling yowl cut off all conversation, followed by a loud hissing and a clatter as though some alien creature had broken in and was tearing up the place.

2

Faith rushed to her desk, where the commotion was coming from.

Marlene and Edna followed on her heels, their voices taut with exclamation.

Faith stared in shock. Watson's feet were planted wide apart on the floor, his body straining forward, ears flattened against his head. His short fur stood on end, and an unearthly growl emanated from his throat. The contents of his bowl and water dish were splayed across the floor.

On a low shelf across from Watson crouched a huge cat with eyes that burned like blue fire. Its mostly white coat was long and ruffled with chocolate-brown markings.

Faith recognized the cat known as a Ragdoll. While the breed was named for its propensity to flop happily into the arms of anyone who picked it up, Faith wouldn't have cared to cradle this distressed animal in her arms at the moment.

"Faja!" Edna sprinted toward the cringing cat. "You naughty cat! How did you get out?" She reached for the flailing animal and secured it under her left arm with her right gripping its jeweled collar. Big glassy stones—red, purple, amber—circled the two-inch leather strap.

The cat's bushy tail swished like a fat feather duster across Edna's dark suit.

At the same time, Faith scooped Watson into her arms and backed away, making soothing sounds in bewildered dismay.

The Ragdoll must have helped itself to whatever was in Watson's bowl and received a less-than-gracious reaction. Watson was usually quite accommodating toward pets who frequently accompanied their masters to the manor, though infringing on his private property in the library had seldom been tested.

The two felines continued to glare at each other, their guttural snarls an unmusical duet.

"I'm sorry. Watson isn't normally like this," Faith said, pulling her tuxedo cat farther from the fray.

"Faja escaped somehow," Edna said in thinly disguised apology. "Fool animal." She sneezed three times as she removed a tissue from the pocket of her suit. "Why he insists on bringing this mangy—"

"What is going on?" a male voice thundered, silencing the frustrated woman's complaint.

Faith turned to see a man in his late thirties marching over to them. He had bushy, dark hair and a shaggy mustache, and he wore a rumpled ecru suit and an oversize bow tie. The man resembled a young Mark Twain, but unlike the famous author, his coal-black eyes were devoid of humor.

The man stopped in front of them, glancing from Edna to the quivering Ragdoll.

"I'm sorry, Mr. Ames. I—" Edna stopped, stifling yet another sneeze. "I had no idea she had slipped out, and then she got into a tussle with the library cat over his food."

Declan Ames grabbed the cat from his assistant's arms, glowering. "I left you with Faja for one minute, and you let her escape? How is a man to tolerate such incompetence—" He stopped in midsentence, as though trying to restrain his temper. Or perhaps he had become aware of Faith and Marlene staring at him.

An uncomfortable silence descended on the library.

Watson squirmed in Faith's arms, then jumped down and strolled away.

Declan stroked the cat's ruffled fur and managed a broad smile that rendered him darkly handsome. "Well, there's no harm done," he said in a soothing baritone. "Do forgive this unwarranted interruption."

"I'm terribly sorry, Mr. Ames," Marlene said. "I'm afraid these things can happen with pets around." She narrowed her eyes at Faith as if blaming her for the entire incident.

Faith swallowed. Marlene's antipathy to cats—Watson in particular—was a given. The assistant manager wasn't about to stand up for her against a guest.

"Not to worry," Declan cut in gallantly. "Faja is quite a homebody. I don't know what got into her to leave that excellent suite of ours." He smiled at Faith. "As for you and your obviously innocent animal, there can be no fault. When a woman loves cats, I am her friend and comrade, without further introduction."

Faith recognized Declan's comment as a slight variation on a well-known Twain quote. She was amused to realize that Declan was acting in character—even in advance of his officially scheduled performance. She cleared her throat. "I think Faja and Watson just surprised each other. Watson is rather territorial where the library and his food dish are concerned."

Cradling the now-limp Ragdoll in his arms, Declan nodded. "Faja and I will leave you in peace, then. Come along, Edna. Let's allow these good people to return to their worthy pursuits."

Edna spun around on her heel and followed Declan and the querulous cat to the library door. She whipped out her tissue again as another sneeze erupted.

"I believe Mr. Ames's assistant has contracted a cold," Faith said to Marlene. "Or else she's allergic to cats." It must have been a trial for the hapless Edna to work so closely with the cat-loving Declan. No doubt she would quickly repair to her quarters to take an antihistamine.

Wolfe Jaxon, the handsome co-owner of Castleton Manor, passed the retreating Declan and Edna as he entered the library, carrying two coffee cups outfitted with cardboard sleeves.

Faith felt a familiar rising somewhere between her stomach and her heart. Wolfe had been away on business for nearly two weeks, but here he was, looking handsome in a tailored gray suit and a tie that matched his devastatingly blue eyes.

After setting the cups down on Faith's desk, Wolfe turned to Marlene. "Was that the Mark Twain impressionist you mentioned?"

"It was," Marlene said without enthusiasm. "Declan Ames and his assistant, Edna Grimmell. Unfortunately, there was a bit of a commotion, but I think we managed to smooth things over."

To Faith's ears, Marlene didn't sound at all convinced. She grimaced. "It was only a little trouble between Declan's cat and Watson. I don't think he was happy about company at his food dish, and the two of them got into a tiff."

"So, the impressionist is a cat lover like Twain," Wolfe remarked with a smile. "I believe the famous author once called cats 'the cleanest, cunningest, and most intelligent things I know, outside of the girl you love, of course.'"

Faith swallowed, her cheeks growing warm. To cover her embarrassment, she said, "Yes, I believe he also said, 'If man could be crossed with the cat it would improve man, but it would deteriorate the cat.'"

"So, all's well that ends well," Wolfe said, his smile broadening.

"One can only hope," Marlene said with a sigh. Then, quickly tucking up the loose threads of her professional demeanor, she checked her clipboard. "I'd like to go over a few things for the retreat with you. How's your schedule this morning?"

"I'll meet you in your office in a few minutes," Wolfe said, consulting his watch.

With a suspect glance at the coffee, Marlene left, shoulders high, back straight, clipboard in hand.

"I'm sorry about all this," Faith said when the library door closed and Marlene's footsteps had receded down the hall.

"Don't worry," Wolfe replied. "These things happen."

Faith met Wolfe's gaze, recalling how his eyes could shine like sun through stained glass. However quirky or difficult the guests of this retreat might be, she felt calm knowing that Wolfe was here and he had brought a cup of coffee just for her.

Wolfe smiled. "It's great to see you."

Faith felt the lump in her throat thicken. She always missed him when he was away on the frequent trips his business required, but this time she had felt a different sort of emptiness. Like part of herself was missing. *That's a dangerous feeling*, she warned herself. She returned his smile. "You too. I hope it was a good trip."

"It was successful, but I'm glad to be back," he said. "I thought we could share a quick cup of coffee."

"That sounds wonderful," Faith said. "But let me put his majesty's domain in order first."

"I'll help." Wolfe followed her to the area behind her desk.

As they wiped up the water and put fresh kibble in Watson's bowl, the cat took up residence on the ledge and watched the proceedings.

"It's good to see you too," Wolfe said, smoothing the soft fur around Watson's ears. "Here's to better mornings," he said with a final pat.

Watson purred in response.

Wolfe sat down in the chair next to Faith's desk and handed one of the cups to her.

Faith sipped the beverage. "Thank you. This is perfect," she murmured.

"It sounds like your morning got off to a rocky start." Wolfe took a drink.

She set the coffee down, keeping her hands wrapped around the warm cup. "Declan Ames isn't exactly what I expected. Do you know him?"

"No. Someone who heard his Twain impression recommended him to Marlene." Wolfe lifted an eyebrow. "Actually, Marlene says that Declan was eager to visit the Cape and he offered his services in exchange for registration at the retreat."

"Really? It sounds like a bargain for us."

Wolfe nodded. "Most of the actors who do impressions ask a great deal more and don't really want to mingle with other guests."

"Hal Holbrook was the classic Twain impressionist," Faith said. "I'm not sure anyone else can quite measure up."

"You make a good point. It'll be interesting to see how Declan portrays him." Wolfe paused, then said, "Declan is younger than I assumed he would be."

"I thought the same thing," Faith said, then frowned. "Surprisingly, he has a heart condition and has to be careful, especially with his diet. He and his assistant are giving Brooke a list of demands, such as no gluten, no salt, and limited sugar."

"A heart patient. I see. Well, I'm sure Brooke will be accommodating." Wolfe smiled and leaned in a little across the desk. "But tell me, how are you?"

"I'm just fine," she said, loving his attentive posture and the way his strong jaw could soften in an instant. She shook herself mentally. She was still amazed at the wave of good fortune that had carried her to Lighthouse Bay and into the graces of this man. She felt her cheeks go warm and hurried to distract her thoughts. "It's so beautiful at the manor in the spring. I could hardly make myself come inside today. Have you seen the tulip trees?"

"I have," he said, laughing softly. "The grounds look spectacular."

The door opened, and two women entered with not-so-quiet exclamations as they viewed the grandeur of the manor's library. A first look at the impressive, walnut-paneled, two-story room often drew astonished reactions from guests.

"Your public awaits," Wolfe said with a wink. He stood and grabbed his coffee cup. "Mine too. I'll see you later."

Faith got up to join the ladies.

The women appeared to be in their early sixties, and they had gray hair and similar facial features. One pointed to the French doors that led out to the terrace. The other ran her fingers lovingly over the carved surfaces of the fireplace.

She smiled at them. "Good morning. I'm Faith Newberry, the

librarian. If there's anything you'd like to know about the library, please feel free to ask."

"Oh, honey, I've never seen such a glorious library," one of the women gushed. She was dressed in vibrant pink, and her eyes sparkled as brightly as the many jewels on her fingers. "I'm Madeline Morrissey from New Haven. I absolutely love this beautiful place."

"I'm her sister, Corinna Morrissey," her companion said in a polite, well-modulated tone. She wore no makeup or jewelry except for a small gold wreath on the lapel of her beige suit. She had strong features and intelligent eyes the color of amber.

A professor, Faith thought, *or maybe the executive director of something. Formidable in any case.*

"We have the Yale Peabody Museum of Natural History, the Yale University Art Gallery, and the Yale Center for British Art at home," Madeline continued. "But I have never seen such a magnificent establishment as this." She gazed around the room and motioned to the small locked glass cases. "I'll bet those hold rare books."

Faith took a step back, but she couldn't help being touched by Madeline's childlike enthusiasm. "They do indeed. And you'll be pleased to know that in addition to the collection of autographed Agatha Christie books, we also have a few Mark Twain first editions."

Madeline gasped. "How wonderful!" Then something across the room seemed to capture the gregarious woman's interest, and she strode away toward Faith's desk and the antique bombé chest near it.

"My sister is somewhat excitable," Corinna admitted in a kind of embarrassed restraint. Her eyes darkened as she watched Madeline's movements. "She is a lover of beautiful things and . . ." Her voice trailed off.

Faith remained silent, waiting for Corinna to continue.

A moment later, Corinna seemed to recover. She smiled. "It's our first visit to this luxurious estate, and I want you to know that we're grateful for the accommodations provided for us. The Jane Austen Suite is more than adequate for our needs."

"That's wonderful to hear," Faith said, happy to praise her employer and his generosity. "This grand mansion has been in the Jaxon family for over a century." When encouraged, she could wax eloquent on the amenities of Lighthouse Bay and the features of Castleton Manor.

"We are very much looking forward to this retreat celebrating American novelists," Corinna said.

Faith nodded. "It should be especially enjoyable and educational. One of our guests is an actor who will portray the renowned Mark Twain for us. It's a surprise addition—not included in the brochure you received. Perhaps you've heard Declan Ames perform? He's from Hartford."

The staid and controlled Morrissey sister appeared startled, her complexion going pale. "No, I hadn't heard he was coming. Excuse me. I should catch up with my sister. She needs her rest." Corinna strode off toward Madeline on slightly wobbly high heels.

The sisters made a hasty exit from the room, with Corinna clutching Madeline's arm and shepherding her out the door.

An eccentric pair, Faith thought. She had met many unusual people since she'd started working at the manor, and most of them had enriched her life in some way. She smiled. Perhaps the sisters thought Castleton Manor's librarian was a little odd too.

When the library emptied of guests, Faith sat down at her desk. It was a grand piece of furniture with its ornate carved legs and sides. The carving included a large cameo featuring some distant Jaxon family ancestor with a wise, discerning face.

She started to collect her thoughts for the presentation she was scheduled to give this evening. It would be an overview of nineteenth-century American literature and what guests could expect to find in the library on the subject.

Watson twined around the legs of the desk and gazed up at her with a question on his face. Then, as though reading permission in her features, he hopped into her lap and curled up into a ball.

She scratched his white bib. "Do you need a little TLC after your encounter with the Ragdoll?"

Watson purred as if in agreement.

"It's certainly been a strange morning," she told him.

Before she could settle into her work, her cell phone jangled.

At the sound, Watson abandoned her lap and abruptly left the room. He was probably in search of a new adventure.

She checked the screen. It was Midge Foster, her good friend and fellow member of the book club. Midge operated Watson's favorite shop, Happy Tails Gourmet Bakery, and she also ran a veterinary practice and made herself available to the pets at the manor when called upon.

"Good morning," Faith said.

"Are you hard at work on the new retreat?" Midge asked. "I don't know how you keep up with all those people coming and going."

"It's a wonderful life," Faith said breezily.

"Sounds like a good title for a movie," Midge quipped.

Faith laughed.

"It sounds like you're in good spirits," Midge remarked. "Wolfe must be back."

Before Faith could reply, her friend added, "Among the people coming and going, have you seen Brooke? I've been trying to reach her since last night."

Faith felt a sudden sense of unease. Brooke hadn't arrived for work at her usual time, and she'd been distracted and quiet lately. It wasn't like her. "No, but I was just about to scrounge a treat from her kitchen to go with my coffee. Why do you ask?"

"I've had Diva at the clinic overnight for observation because Brooke was worried about her angelfish. Says she's off her feed and moping around."

"Oh no," Faith said. That could explain her friend's behavior.

Brooke doted on her two angelfish, Diva and Bling. She even projected her own emotions onto them, especially where men were concerned. She swore that Diva and Bling could spot a loser a mile away. "How's Diva doing?"

"The little darling is perfectly fine," Midge said, slipping into her distinctive Southern accent. "She's swimming at lightning speed and nibbling everything in sight. Brooke should come and get her before Bling gets too lonesome."

"That should make her day," Faith said. "I'll let her know right away."

After Faith disconnected, she put her cell phone in her pocket and tapped her fingers on her desk. No patrons were in the library, so she could slip out for a few minutes. She would just tuck away her notes. But where was the paperweight she always kept on the corner of her desk?

The paperweight was nothing special and certainly not valuable—to anyone but her. Her father had given her the oval globe with tiny gold-and-green flowers around its edge. In the center, he had inserted a sepia replica of her grandmother's face.

She scanned her desk and the adjacent chest that served as a credenza, but the paperweight was nowhere to be seen. She must have put it in a drawer. She decided to look later. Right now, she needed to talk to Brooke.

Faith went downstairs to the basement. She found Brooke sitting at the small table in the back corner of the kitchen.

"Hey," Faith called as she approached.

Brooke glanced up with a start and dropped the pencil onto the page in front of her. "You startled me," she said, her forehead wrinkling. She tucked a strand of platinum hair behind her ear and sat up straighter in her chair. Her white chef's apron hung untied from her shoulders as though she hadn't had the energy to remove it completely when she sat down.

Faith hesitated at her friend's frazzled appearance. "I'm sorry."

She studied Brooke's strained features. Perhaps she hadn't slept well. "Are you all right?"

"Of course," she said, attempting a smile that didn't quite reach her eyes. "I've just been up to my ears with these menus and special-diet requests. There's so much to do."

"Ah, did Marlene bring the formidable Edna Grimmell to see you?"

Brooke nodded. "It's to be expected, I suppose, though usually I get these requests in advance of a guest's arrival instead of at the last minute."

"I understand Mr. Ames is a heart patient," Faith said. "It puts the administration in something of an awkward position because it makes them vulnerable if something should happen. I guess he's hoping for a therapeutic retreat at the manor."

"It sounds presumptuous to me," Brooke said, her expression bordering on scornful.

"But to his credit," Faith continued, stifling her surprise, "he's offering to give a professional impersonation of Mark Twain without asking the fee actors like him usually get."

Brooke didn't respond.

"By the way, he's quite handsome." Faith watched for the familiar spark of interest. Brooke was a hopeless romantic, and she was always the one to choose a romance novel for their book club's next read.

Brooke stared off into space as though completely preoccupied.

Faith drew in a breath. Maybe Brooke was more worried about her pet angelfish than anyone thought. "Midge asked me to tell you that Diva is just fine. You can pick her up and take her home anytime. I'm sure Bling has been lonely without her."

Brooke looked at Faith, but she appeared not to have heard.

"She says Diva's appetite is more than adequate and that she's swimming around happy as a clam." She grinned at Brooke, desperate to break through her malaise. "How happy *is* a clam, do you think?"

"Oh," Brooke said, pushing back her chair and getting up. "That's really good news. I was afraid something was wrong. You know how sensitive my Diva can be." She flung the apron aside, revealing a cerulean-blue wraparound dress.

"Any more of those marvelous macaroons you made the other day?" Faith asked, heading for a counter on which several stacked tins were arranged. She found herself craving something gooey and sweet.

"Help yourself," Brooke said.

"Watson and I have had a stressful morning," Faith added as she packed a few treats into a small box.

"I'm sorry," Brooke said without her usual sparkle.

Faith outlined the kerfuffle with Declan's Ragdoll cat. She thought her rendition of the scene was worthy of a laugh or two, but Brooke only managed a small smile.

"Are you sure you're all right?" Faith prodded gently.

"I'm sorry," Brooke said. "I'm just tired. Thanks for telling me about Diva."

"Sure." Faith held up the box. "Thanks for the macaroons. They'll soothe my ruffled nerves and keep me sane for a little while longer."

Faith returned to the library with a nagging sense that all was not well with Brooke.

3

The cat took his time going home from the library. He stopped in the lovely herb garden, where a variety of delightful scents made his nose twitch with anticipation.

He knew that the human who took care of the trees and flowers always planted an assortment of herbs that magically appeared when the air turned warm. One plant made him feel downright giddy, and he could certainly do with a little cheering up after tangling with that dastardly interloper.

The nerve of that long-haired snoop who invaded his private domain! Even after being asked to vacate the premises, the nasty feline went right on nibbling his favorite morning snack. He had asked politely. Well, as politely as a superior cat who is being robbed can manage. Everyone knew that tuxedos were the most handsome of all their kind, with white bibs and spats—stunning complements to their shiny black coats. Moreover, they had superior intelligence—a differential of some 200 percent over other cats. His own human had said so.

He paused to take a long sniff of the balmy air. Was that it—the delicacy he was searching for? Oh yes, there was the green and lush plant. Feeling like a kitten again, he began to kick up his heels. He plunged his nose into the delectable substance. Soon he found himself licking and chewing, shaking his chin, and rubbing his face in its minty depths in a most undignified manner. Ah, heaven!

Wait! He wasn't alone. People sounds. There was the human who often came to visit at his cottage. She was the one who cooked all those delicious meals. The cat could always depend on her for a handout when his own human wasn't looking. Maybe he'd scamper over and say hello.

He rolled out of his little patch of paradise, hoping he hadn't been *observed carrying on like a common alley cat, and crept stealthily through the garden. But then he inched back.*

Another human who had been partially hidden under a topiary stepped out along the path. It was the one that belonged to that raggedy cat who had stolen his food.

The cat's growl started low in his throat as he watched. The human in the funny bow tie rested a hand on the other's arm and said something. His friend of the delicious meals was talking too, shaking her head, and stepping back. Then she broke away and ran.

The owner of the uppity cat stood watching the other human go. After a few moments, he shrugged and walked down the path, making the silly sound humans made with their mouths when their eyes were happy. But this human didn't look happy at all.

The cat hunkered down and flattened his ears. Was the fluffy feline thief waiting for his owner in the bushes?

But no cat appeared. There was only the tall human shuffling along the path.

The cat started to skulk after him. A good scratch on the person's leg might just make up for the morning's shenanigans. And for scaring one of his favorite humans.

But the tantalizing minty scent wafted over him again, and he began to feel sleepy. His cottage with its comfy spot on the couch awaited.

It was time to go home.

When Faith returned to the cottage after closing the library, she found Watson curled up on the couch.

The tuxedo cat was in high spirits—snuggling and rolling and purring to beat the band.

"What's put you in such a good mood?" Faith asked, chucking him under the chin. She sniffed at his fur. "I'll bet you found some catnip, didn't you?" The gardeners always planted a plot of catnip in the herb garden for the manor's feline guests.

She was rewarded by a sleepy slit of green eye and raspy sounds of contentment.

"At least you seem to have forgotten about your tangle with that pretty Ragdoll." Faith smiled as she sat down next to him, resting a moment before she returned to the manor for the retreat's opening event.

Marlene had asked Faith to attend dinner with the guests. After the meal, Faith was scheduled to give a brief presentation on nineteenth-century literature, and then the attendees would be treated to light refreshments.

Faith poured kibble into Watson's bowl and refilled his water.

The cat got up to eat his food. Then he immediately returned to his spot on the couch.

Checking the clock, she realized she'd better hurry if she wanted to arrive on time for dinner. She dressed in a pale-aqua dress and a light shawl. Usually, she wore her hair loose around her shoulders, but in the spirit of nineteenth-century fashion, she styled it in a French twist, letting a few wispy tendrils cascade around her face.

"See you after the program," she told Watson, and she slipped out of the cottage.

As she walked the path to the manor, she wondered about Brooke's strange behavior. She hoped she'd find a moment to talk to her tonight.

Faith spoke to a few guests when she entered the manor and headed to the dining room.

"Ah, there you are finally," Marlene intoned.

Faith stifled a sigh. She was twenty minutes early, but it was normal for the assistant manager to fuss and worry. No detail must be overlooked. Nothing short of perfection would do. Faith applauded this efficiency, but there were times when it irked her all the same.

"The Morrissey sisters have asked you to join them for dinner," Marlene said. She ushered Faith over to the sisters' table, then left.

Faith greeted Madeline and Corinna as she sat down. "I hope you two are enjoying your stay so far."

"It's delightful." Madeline beamed. "I never want to go home."

"I'm looking forward to your presentation," Corinna added.

"Thank you," Faith said. "I hope you'll enjoy it."

Further conversation was interrupted when their salads were served.

Faith glanced around for Brooke, but she didn't see her. She assumed she was still busy in the kitchen.

As the main course of salmon and garlic-roasted potatoes was passed out, a pair of latecomers sat down at their table and engaged the sisters in conversation.

Faith joined their lively discussion about writers, and the rest of the meal passed quickly.

Right before dessert was handed out, Faith excused herself and hurried to the library. She wanted to make sure it had been readied for the event.

When she entered the room, she was pleased with the atmosphere. The guests would take their places on the comfortable couches and chairs in front of the fireplace. A low fire had been lit against the chill that still held sway on April evenings along the coast. Lights glowed from overhead chandeliers and wall sconces in the expansive two-story room. The flames lent a reddish-gold ambience, fitting for Victorian reminiscence. Hyacinth, tulip, and white lilac arrangements graced the mantel and occasional tables.

Faith retrieved her leather binder from her desk and checked her notes.

Marlene walked over to her. "Is everything set?"

"Yes, and I have my notes right here." Faith held up the binder.

"Remember to keep it light and brief. No getting carried away." Marlene jutted her chin forward. "I know how you are when it comes to books."

"Don't worry," Faith said. "I'll do my best not to bore our guests."

"Well, I assume I have found the right venue for tonight's event," a deep voice boomed.

Faith turned to see a fortyish barrel-chested man with sandy hair—thin on top and redistributed in thick sideburns. Pale brows arched over blue eyes flecked with brown. He wore a Western-style jacket over a white shirt and a string tie. A silver-buckled belt strained against his girth.

"Yes, you have found the right place," Marlene said. "And our librarian, Miss Newberry, will be getting things started soon." She turned to Faith. "Let me introduce you to Professor Clement George."

"It's nice to meet you, ma'am," he said, extending a big hand.

Faith shook the proffered hand. "It's nice to meet you too."

"Did you find everything to your satisfaction?" Marlene asked him.

"It will do just fine," Clement replied as he gazed around the room. He rocked forward slightly. "Quite an elegant library you have here."

Faith saw that in addition to designer jeans he was wearing cowboy boots. *All he needs is a Stetson,* she thought.

"Professor George is a member of the Bergen Historical Society outside greater Hartford," Marlene said by way of further introduction. "A few of the other guests hold membership in the society, including Declan Ames and Madeline and Corinna Morrissey."

Faith nodded. It was only natural that Mark Twain enthusiasts would be found in such a society near Hartford, given that it housed the Twain home and museum. How appropriate that they would be treated to an appearance by the famous author in the form of Declan Ames.

As though he had heard his name in Faith's thoughts, the actor strolled up behind Clement. "Bending the ladies' ears to your latest project, are you, Professor?" Declan said with an upward twist of his mustached mouth. The inclusion of "professor" sounded gratuitous. His humorless dark eyes were as cold as the Atlantic in spring.

Clement took a step back in apparent surprise and faced the shorter man.

"One could argue whether the subject is worth the paper expended to produce it," Declan said. He gave a little bow as though to soften the sting of his insult. "Mind you, I'm just repeating the sentiment of the most important figure in American literature, and we all know what Mr. Twain thought of your subject."

Faith frowned at Declan's remarks. She wondered what she might say to ease the situation.

Before she could respond, Clement said, "The jury's still out on whether the man you try to imitate truly holds the most important place in nineteenth-century literature as you propose. It just so happens that Bret Harte is enjoying a resurgence of popularity—and with good reason."

Faith had read that Twain and Harte had once been friends and later had a falling-out. No one was quite sure what had caused their love-hate relationship. She glanced from Declan to Clement and felt an animosity that made her shiver.

Marlene broke in, addressing Faith. "Professor George is a scholar of Victorian literature. I believe he's writing a new biography of Bret Harte." She turned to Clement. "Is that correct?"

"Indeed. Harte is a Midas of the pen and a literary prince of the Gilded Age." He drew himself up to his full six-foot-plus height.

Faith recalled a couple of Harte's famous stories that she had enjoyed: "The Luck of Roaring Camp" and "The Outcasts of Poker Flat." Some experts credited Harte with reinventing the American short story and laying the foundation for the Western.

"Harte was a worldwide celebrity author," Clement went on, his expression daring anyone to disagree. "Henry Adams considered him one of the most brilliant men of his time."

"Or more likely 'the most contemptible, poor little soulless blatherskite that exists on the planet today,'" Declan said with another mock bow. "Those were Twain's words—not mine, my good fellow."

An uncomfortable silence descended.

Declan stroked his mustache as though in contemplation. "Maybe you should consider another project, Professor." He paused, raising his dark brows meaningfully. "Something you can rightfully claim as yours, that is." With those inscrutable words, the actor strode away.

Declan had been surprisingly rude, and Faith felt sorry for Clement.

Marlene broke through the uncomfortable tension. She gestured to the guests filing into the room. "I believe it's time to get started. I think we should all take our seats." She steered Faith to the fireplace, where a small podium had been set up facing the couches and chairs.

When the guests were seated, Faith greeted them with a smile, hoping to put them at ease. She noticed that Declan and Clement sat as far away from each other as possible. How odd that these two members of the same historical society who appeared to know each other also mimicked the conflict between Twain and Harte. She hoped both men would keep civil tongues in their heads for the remainder of the retreat.

"I know you're going to enjoy this very special retreat featuring American novels of the nineteenth century," Faith began. "Here in Castleton's library you'll find works by some well-known favorites in addition to some lesser-known stars who may surprise you."

The door creaked open.

Glancing up, Faith recognized the two late arrivals—the sisters she'd just had dinner with. She idly wondered what had held them up.

Faith nodded a welcome to Madeline and Corinna as they quietly slipped into chairs in the last row.

No doubt embarrassed, they did not acknowledge her and kept their heads down.

Faith cleared her throat and launched into her subject. "In the nineteenth century, American writers forged a path to achieve cultural independence from the old ways. They chronicled political and religious revolts and the difficulties of building a society in a continent that was still untamed." Her gaze connected with Clement, who no doubt resonated with writings of the Western frontier—Bret Harte in particular.

"By the middle of the century, many writers focused on the issue of slavery," Faith continued. "Some writers commented on the rise of materialism in their novels. Other writers, such as Mark Twain, responded by turning back to the South of the past." She glanced in Declan's direction and hurried on. "The harsh conditions of large cities were also topics of examination. You may want to explore some of these nineteenth-century literati while you're here."

A few minutes later, the library door opened. Laura Kettrick signaled shyly to Faith that the refreshments were ready in the salon.

Faith was surprised to see the somewhat clumsy but eager young housekeeper handling the refreshments. Normally, Brooke officiated over the evening soirees. Faith had assumed that Brooke was busy in the kitchen during dinner, but perhaps she had another engagement tonight.

She nodded to Laura to indicate that they were almost ready.

As Faith wrapped up her presentation, she worried anew about Brooke's unusual behavior. She seemed to be hiding herself away from the manor guests.

When the presentation was over and the crowd began exiting the room, Faith went to slip her notes into her lower desk drawer. She was surprised to find her paperweight inside the drawer. It must have fallen into the drawer when she cleared her desk. She shrugged, momentarily puzzled, but there was no time to give it further thought.

She hurried to the salon, where everyone was milling around the refreshments table spread with fancy hors d'oeuvres and a variety of tempting sweets.

Laura poured the coffee with a slight tremble of her fingers. She always seemed afraid of spilling hot liquid on the guests.

Faith stepped up beside her. "You're doing great," she whispered in her ear. "Where's Brooke? I wanted to talk to her, but I didn't see her at dinner."

"She had to leave," Laura replied.

"Is there something wrong?" Faith asked.

Before Laura could answer, Declan walked up to them. He declined a plate but accepted a cup of black coffee. "And where is that wonderful chef who prepared such a delicious supper to my specific requirements?" he asked, scanning the room.

"She's not here," Laura responded softly. "But I'm sure she'll be back in the morning."

Declan raised his eyebrows, then sauntered away.

Suddenly, a gasp arose as an animal streaked into the room.

It was Faja—Declan's Ragdoll—and chasing after her was Edna, black hair falling over her eyes. Her heels clattered as she sprinted in a skirt too tight for strenuous activity. When Faja leaped onto a chair, Edna snatched up the cat and secured her in her arms.

Declan spun around and marched over to his assistant. "What is going on? I leave Faja in your charge for an hour, and look what you've—" His face flushed red, then seemed to drain to a pasty white. "And where in thunder is her collar?"

Indeed, the gaudy jeweled collar was gone from the Ragdoll's neck. The cat seemed quite pleased with its absence and let herself go limp and contented in Edna's arms.

Faith couldn't help but smile, recalling that the Ragdoll breed is notable for collapsing into the arms of anyone who holds them, even if they are cradled on their backs. They were known for their docility, but they were an active breed too, as Faja had already demonstrated.

"I asked you, where is Faja's collar?" Declan repeated. "Someone stole it. I demand that the culprit show himself." He turned and glared at everyone in the room.

"Please calm down," Edna cajoled. "Don't forget about your blood pressure—"

Her words were cut short as Wolfe strode toward them, carrying Faja's jeweled collar. He was followed by Midge, whose white vet's coat flagged open over her blouse and jeans.

"What? What in—" Declan sputtered, glancing at Wolfe, then at his assistant.

Edna cringed, displaying none of the haughty bravado she had shown earlier.

"Is there a problem here?" Wolfe demanded, his steely gaze locked on Declan.

"I-I—" Declan rubbed a hand over his mustache as though to make sense of a puzzle or gain control of himself. "I left Faja in my assistant's care, and she has apparently allowed my cat to get out and run all over the place." He lowered his voice. "I do apologize for the trouble she has caused, but—" He broke off again and gazed around in bewilderment.

"Your assistant requested the aid of our concierge veterinarian a little while ago," Wolfe said. "Dr. Foster had to remove the cat's collar, and in the process, the cat broke away and ran." He handed the collar to Ames.

"I apologize for the trouble, sir," Midge said, drawing up alongside Wolfe. "Miss Grimmell thought Faja had eaten something off the floor, and she was afraid the cat would choke. I was called in to assist. Fortunately, it was a false alarm." She reached across Edna to pet Faja's head. "I assure you that your cat is all right."

Declan seized the cat and turned to leave the room. He glared behind him at Edna, his face flushed with anger, black eyes blazing.

Unnerved by the man's over-the-top reaction, Faith stared after him. For the first time, she felt sorry for his hapless assistant.

4

The next morning, Faith pulled a batch of triple-berry muffins from the oven. Her aunt had promised to stop by the cottage on her way to the Candle House Library in town, and Midge had said she might be able to join them.

Faith caught the muffins just in time. They were a touch browner than she liked, but an early phone call from Wolfe had taken her mind off baking.

"I'm sorry I didn't make it back in time for your presentation last night," he had said. "How did it go?"

"It went all right, I think," she said. She hadn't seen Wolfe last night until the refreshments were served in the salon. After Wolfe confronted Declan, he'd disappeared to confer with Edna. She pictured him now, probably already at his desk and attacking the day's demands.

"Sorry about that business over the cat last night," Wolfe said. "Sometimes allowing pets at these retreats is risky."

"But you arrived just in time," she said. "I was afraid our Twain impressionist might have a coronary when that cat came flying into the room with Edna chasing her."

"Things are never dull around here, are they?" he quipped. He was quiet for a long moment, then added, "I didn't get a chance to tell you, but you looked beautiful last night."

She swallowed. His unexpected compliment derailed her. "And you looked like an avenging angel in a business suit," she told him. "You sure stopped Declan in his tracks."

Now, as she sprinkled coarse sugar crystals over the muffins, she thought about her friendship with Wolfe. It had blossomed as naturally as the rhododendrons flanking her cottage. And as sweetly.

She felt a surprising lump in her throat and shook herself mentally. *Back to earth*, she scolded herself. *Eileen will be here any minute.*

Faith arranged the muffins on one of her favorite serving plates, a Delft Blue hexagon that her mother had given her for her birthday. She had always admired the intricate pattern of flowers and shapes that covered its gleaming surface. It coordinated well with the blue-and-white decor in her light, airy kitchen.

She loved everything about her home, a completely renovated gardener's cottage near enough to the ocean to enjoy its soft susurrations, which often lulled her to sleep at night.

Watson, who had perched on a chair for a closer look at the savory muffins, leaped down at the sound of a car approaching the cottage.

Faith peered out the window to see Eileen Piper climb out of her car. The sight of her favorite aunt was good compensation for having to end her conversation with Wolfe.

Being near her mother's widowed sister had been one of the biggest pluses in her decision to come to Lighthouse Bay. They had formed a close bond and shared a love of books—especially mysteries. They had even solved a few with the help of the other Candle House Book Club members.

Faith rushed to fling open the door and throw her arms around her aunt. "I'm so glad to see you," she said, helping her with her jacket and the knitting tote that she never went anywhere without. Despite her painful rheumatoid arthritis, Eileen managed to craft some of the most beautiful and intricate items Faith had ever seen.

"I have some free time this morning, and I couldn't think of a better way to spend it," Eileen said, rearranging her shoulder-length brown hair. The style was easy and unpretentious, swept off her forehead.

Watson glanced up at Eileen, then twined around her ankles.

"Of course I was referring to you too," Eileen told him as she scratched behind his ears.

The cat purred in response.

"Is that triple-berry muffins I smell?" Eileen asked. Without waiting for an answer, she pressed forward into the kitchen with an eager step.

"I think I left them in the oven a tad too long, but they should be fine with a little butter," Faith said as she followed.

Eileen sat down at the table, then unfolded a flowered napkin and spread it over her lap. "They smell delicious. I'll take two, and hold the butter."

Faith laughed. She retrieved plates from the cupboard and set them on the table. Then she poured two cups of coffee and handed one to her aunt.

"Thank you, dear," Eileen said. She helped herself to a muffin and took a bite. "Excellent."

"I'm glad you came over today," Faith said as she reached for a muffin.

"Me too. Things have been so busy at the library, and we haven't had a chance to talk. I'm dying to hear what's going on in your life. Is Wolfe back?"

"He is," Faith said. "I was talking to him right before you arrived."

"Ah," Eileen said, eyes twinkling, "the reason you burned the muffins."

"They're not burned—just nicely browned," Faith protested. She gave her aunt a warning look.

Eileen laughed. "I'm only teasing you. You know I couldn't be happier if you and Wolfe got together. He's a good man. And your muffins are just the way I like them." She took another bite. "Now tell me how things are going at the retreat."

Faith sighed, wondering where to begin with the whirlwind first hours of the retreat. "It's been interesting."

"I heard that sigh," Eileen said. "Did your guest who does impressions of Mark Twain arrive?"

Faith drew in her breath as she recalled the actor's rude comments and brash behavior. She was aware of her aunt's perceptive gaze. "He's here. We met quite by accident in the library yesterday morning before the retreat even began." She glanced at Watson, who was sunning himself on the windowsill. "It wasn't the most auspicious of beginnings for Watson."

"What happened?" Eileen asked. She sipped her coffee.

Faith briefly recounted the tale of Declan Ames and his cat, Faja.

Eileen put her cup down. "Oh no, two cats fighting in the library. And your Twain impressionist sounds rather temperamental and a little hard on his assistant. I hope he pays her well."

"I hope so too. I'm pretty sure she's allergic to cats." Faith recalled Edna's sniffs and sneezes as she corralled the runaway animal. "She seems devoted to Declan, though. She had Marlene running in circles to make sure he's properly housed and fed while he's here. Apparently, he's been on a special diet ever since he had a heart attack last year."

Eileen raised her eyebrows. "A heart attack? Is he an elderly man?"

"He's not even forty and, on the surface, more handsome than is good for him."

"You don't like him," Eileen said with a note of surprise.

"It's not that I don't like him. I don't really know him." Faith hesitated, not wanting to disparage him, especially when all the facts weren't known. "But he was rather rude to another guest."

"Who was that?"

"A Bret Harte enthusiast named Clement George who's working on a new biography of the writer," Faith answered. "He's a member of that historical society near Hartford."

"I knew a Clement George," Eileen said.

"Really?"

"Yes, there was a Professor George connected with a private college outside of Boston. Very elite." Eileen was quiet for a moment, evidently recollecting. "We never talked in person, but we had a few phone conversations related to the research he was doing at the time. He needed old literary documents from Candle House."

"So you don't know what he looks like?" Faith asked.

"I've seen a picture of him," Eileen said. "He was a big man with a big chest."

"That sounds like him. His hair is thinning on top, but he's got some major sideburns." Faith smiled, adding, "They go well with his string tie and cowboy boots."

"One and the same. I'd bet on it," Eileen said as she took another muffin.

"When did you talk to him?"

"It was more than a decade ago," Eileen said. "I haven't heard anything about him recently, and I always wondered what happened to him."

"I'm not sure whether he's still teaching or not," Faith said. "But I do know that Declan isn't a fan."

"Interesting. It seems like your Mark Twain impressionist and the Bret Harte aficionado are continuing the historic feud between the two authors. Maybe it's part of the act."

If that was the case, Faith had to admit they played their parts well.

Watson suddenly jumped down from the windowsill and ran to the front door.

"My word, if your Watson isn't better than a watchdog," Eileen said. "I hope that's Midge. You said she might drop in."

"I'm sure it's her," Faith said as she and Eileen went to the foyer.

As soon as Faith opened the door, Watson raced out to greet Midge.

Midge transferred her veterinary bag from one arm to the other and bent down to pet Watson. "I'm sorry, but I'm fresh out of tunaroons today," she told him. "I'll have to give you a rain check." Tunaroons were Watson's favorite treat at Midge's pet bakery.

"We were hoping you'd stop by," Faith told her. "I have a nicely browned muffin with your name on it if you're hungry."

Eileen gave Midge a hug. "The muffins are delicious. I've already eaten two of them."

"Then you've eaten one for me," Midge remarked. "My hips

started blooming at the aroma alone. Besides, I'd like to come in, but I'm running late."

"Where are you off to?" Eileen asked.

"The stables. You could walk over there with me, and we could catch up on the way." Midge glanced down at Watson, who was washing his face. "You too."

The cat stopped grooming and looked at her.

"A walk sounds good to me," Faith said. "It's a gorgeous spring day."

Eileen grabbed her jacket from the foyer. "Let's go."

They walked together down the path. It was an unusually balmy day, and birds called out as they flitted from one blossoming tree to the next.

Watson took off ahead of them, and soon his bobbed tail disappeared.

"T. S. Eliot said that April was the cruelest month," Faith said. "But today at least it's tender and warm and just about perfect. Especially since I'm in the company of my good friends."

"Too bad Brooke isn't with us," Eileen commented. "Then we could have called this an official meeting of the book club."

Faith turned to Midge. "I assume she picked Diva up."

Midge narrowed her eyes. "She did, but she seemed preoccupied. I was hoping we could run over to Snickerdoodles, but she said she didn't have time. She left in a hurry."

"I thought she was just worried about her angelfish, but now I'm not so sure." Faith chewed her lip thoughtfully. "She's been staying in the kitchen all the time. She even had Laura serving our guests last night. If I didn't know better, I'd think she was avoiding everyone."

"That doesn't sound like our Brooke," Eileen said, idly picking a blossom from a low-hanging magnolia and tucking it into a buttonhole on her jacket. "You don't think she's sick, do you?"

"Maybe she's in love again," Midge suggested. "No," she quickly amended. "She'd tell us about that."

As they walked on, Faith recalled her conversation with Brooke.

Was she just imagining it, or was there some reason for her reluctance to enter into the spirit of this retreat like she usually did? Faith shook her head. She was probably reading too much into it. After all, everyone was entitled to an off day or a secret or two.

As they rounded the corner, Faith noticed a man wearing jeans and a denim shirt, brushing his mount with slow, determined strokes. The magnificent animal barely moved as the man worked. She admired the horse's mahogany coat gleaming in the sun and its handsome black legs and tail. "Looks like someone has one of the horses out," she said.

"That's the retreat guest who brought his own horse," Midge said. "Marlene told me he trucked a bay here all the way from Cornwall, Connecticut."

"Now that's a devoted equine lover," Eileen said.

In the past, Castleton had hosted some unusual pets—such as a hedgehog, a ferret, and a large number of rabbits—but Faith couldn't recall anyone bringing a horse before. There was really no need to because guests had plenty of the manor's horses to choose from if they wanted to go riding during their stay.

The man was facing away from them, but Faith recognized the height and girth of Clement George, even if he hadn't also been wearing boots and a cowboy hat. Which he was.

Clement turned at the sound of their voices and raised a hand in greeting.

"It's him," Eileen said, stopping on the path. "That's the professor we were talking about, Faith. He's aged some, but he's just as I remember him from his picture."

Clement set his grooming brush down and came toward them, removing his cowboy hat. He smiled at Faith. "The librarian—Miss Newberry, right?" He extended a large hand across the fence.

"Yes, hello," Faith said, shaking his hand.

"I'm Midge Foster, the veterinarian." She held up her veterinary bag as if to confirm it. "Is your bay doing all right with the quarter horses?"

"He's doing fine. And thank you very much." Clement offered his hand to Midge.

Midge shook his hand. "I'm glad to hear it. Please excuse me as I attend to my duties inside the stable." As she walked away, she told Faith and Eileen, "You go on. I'll catch up with you later."

Faith put a hand on her aunt's arm. "This is Eileen Piper, my aunt," she told Clement. "She's the librarian at the Candle House Library in town."

He nodded. "Candle House is a fine old establishment. Dates back to the early 1800s, if I'm not mistaken."

"Yes," Eileen said, always eager to proclaim the praises of the library. "The building retains many of the characteristics of the old candle house where tallow was once processed. It still has some of the original glass in the windows. You must come and see it."

Clement paused. "Beautiful morning for a walk," he finally remarked, obviously trying to change the subject.

Faith wondered if Clement remembered talking to Eileen about his research. If so, she thought he would have mentioned it.

"Are you still at Heatherstone College?" Eileen asked, looking up. Way up. Eileen was a diminutive woman, and Clement was well over six feet. "My late husband was most interested in your work on Elizabethan poets."

Clement seemed stunned by the question and colored slightly. "Well, that was some time ago, but I'm honored that you remember." He tapped his hat against his thigh in what might be a nervous gesture and looked off to one side. "I'm engaged in another study altogether at present. Very absorbing."

"Bret Harte, right?" Eileen responded quickly, blue eyes twinkling. "My niece mentioned the biography you're working on. When I was growing up, I loved 'The Luck of Roaring Camp.' I suggest it to many of the students who come into the library. I wish more of them were interested in the classic stories, but—" She stopped and sighed. "It's hard competing with superheroes from comic books and such."

Clement took a step back toward the waiting bay. "Better get back to currying Beau. The creature expects a certain amount of TLC, whether he's at home or not." He replaced the cowboy hat and smiled, but the eyes beneath his sandy brows retained an odd sense of detachment. "It was good to meet you."

As Faith and Eileen set out for the cottage, Watson appeared at their side.

"Have you been visiting the animals at the kennels?" Faith asked him.

Watson trotted alongside Faith as she and Eileen walked down the steps to the water.

After a few minutes, they stopped to watch the waves lap along the shore.

Watson particularly enjoyed snooping along the edge. He went just close enough to avoid getting his feet wet.

"Professor George is an odd fellow, isn't he?" Eileen commented. "Oh, I know, a lot of academic types can be eccentric, but he seems to have adopted the appearance of Bret Harte, who was fascinated by the Western frontier."

"He even wears cowboy boots and string ties, and he brought a horse to the retreat," Faith said. She tossed a small stone into the water and watched the tide swallow it. "Harte is captivating, I suppose. I read that after his sensational breakthrough, he came to symbolize the self-made literary man."

"He was something of a fugitive from home, though," Eileen added. "He was born in New York but fled to Europe. There's a good deal of speculation about him. Particularly about his love-hate relationship with Mark Twain."

"I didn't see much of the love part yesterday," Faith responded. "But like you said, it could be part of a scheme the two cooked up for this retreat. We might find out tonight during Twain's performance."

"You'll have to let me know how it goes," Eileen said. "Will Clement be giving a presentation?"

"I understand he'll lecture later in the week about his literary hero."

They started walking again, and Watson raced ahead of them.

"Well, would you look at that?" Eileen exclaimed, stopping to stare at a woman who had just rounded a corner onto the main path. "I believe that lady has a cat on a leash."

Faith recognized Edna and Faja. Edna wore a beige blouse, pants, and dress shoes hardly conducive to walking on damp ground and pebbles. Her dark hair swung forward as she stepped carefully, trying to commandeer the cat, who obviously did not approve of being tethered.

Faja squirmed and shook her head, wheezing uncomfortably.

"The ever-dutiful Edna Grimmell," Faith said. It was strange to see her out here, but perhaps she was on her way to visit the horses as some guests liked to do. Faith pondered the puzzling behavior of Declan's assistant as a man walked past them.

"Is that one of your retreat guests?" Eileen asked.

Faith glanced up. She'd been so engrossed in thought that she hadn't really noticed. She squinted in the sunlight as the man turned toward the stables. He was of medium height and slight build. A dark cap obscured the color of his hair, and she hadn't been able to see his face. "I'm not sure. He could be, or maybe he's the new wrangler Samuel hired."

"So that's Declan's assistant walking a cat." Eileen gestured to the squirming feline. "Is that Faja?"

Faith nodded.

"You don't see many cats being taken for a walk." Eileen laughed, resuming her pace as the distance between them narrowed.

"Hello," Faith called to Edna. "And how is Faja today?" She tried not to let her incredulity show. Watson wouldn't put up with a leash, even for a barrel of tunaroons.

"She's fine," Edna said. "Thank you."

As Faith introduced Eileen and Edna, Watson returned from whatever adventure he had found on the beach and stood next to Faith.

At the sight of Watson, Edna quickly pulled Faja back until there was no more give in the leash.

Watson sat down, a curious, almost sad expression on his whiskered face as he stared at Faja.

Edna appeared wary while she observed the two cats, and she held more tightly to the Ragdoll's leash.

"It's certainly a lovely day for a walk," Faith said, pretending not to notice Edna's nervousness.

Edna sneezed. "Yes, nice day," she said, looking miserable. "Mr. Ames likes Faja to have a good airing every day. Nice to see you." She hurried away, extending the long leash, the Ragdoll padding reluctantly behind.

When they were out of earshot, Eileen said drolly, "Eccentricities abound."

"I can hardly wait for tonight."

5

After Faith returned from her walk with Eileen, she opened the library and caught up on correspondence and filing.

The library was quiet while a local women's auxiliary presented a nineteenth-century fashion show for the retreat guests. Faith had seen the excellent presentation, revealing the many changes in costume that occurred from the early 1800s until the close of the century. She knew there were plenty of bustles and petticoats, bonnets and top hats.

"I'm sure they're having quite a time," she said to Watson, who was napping on one of the chairs in front of the fireplace.

Watson glanced up and yawned, then closed his eyes again.

Faith laughed. "Never mind," she said, stroking his sleek fur. "Go back to sleep."

After dinner tonight, the group would enjoy an evening performance by Declan Ames as the venerable Mark Twain. For the sake of harmony, she decided that Watson would have to stay at the cottage during the event.

Patrons began trickling into the library after the fashion show, and Faith spent the rest of the day answering questions and helping them find books.

As Faith worked, she anticipated Declan's evening performance with curiosity and a sense of dread she couldn't explain. She didn't have to like the actor's behavior to appreciate whatever giftedness he might display, did she?

The guests deserved an enjoyable and educational experience, and she hoped they wouldn't be disappointed.

When the last patron had left, Faith gathered her things, then glanced over at Watson. "Ready to go home? We have just enough time for dinner before the performance."

At the mention of food, Watson's ears perked up, and he bounded to the door.

She laughed as she followed him. They rushed to the cottage, where Faith poured kibble into Watson's bowl and refreshed his water.

While Watson crunched his food, Faith had a Greek salad and a glass of iced tea. She usually attended dinners at the manor, but tonight she'd decided to eat a quick bite at home. The program would be held in the library, and Marlene wanted Faith to be there early to give guests an opportunity to browse the shelves before Declan began his presentation. She didn't have any time to waste.

Faith tidied up the kitchen, then changed into a black A-line dress. On the way out the door, she gave Watson a pat on the head and a tunaroon. "Be good. I'll be back soon," she promised.

As she made her way back to the manor, she walked through the Victorian garden, where spring was already working its magic. She could hardly wait for the daffodil festival, but that wouldn't take place until May.

Faith would have to settle for picking a few of the yellow flowers that bloomed along the edge of the garden. Were they daffodils or jonquils? Or were those terms interchangeable? She plucked a small bunch for her desk and hurried on.

She entered the manor and headed straight to the library, where she unlocked the door and set the flowers on her desk.

Faith glanced around the room, noting that everything seemed to be in order. The small podium she'd used last night for her presentation was set up in front of the couches and chairs again, and a raised dais had been placed near the podium. An easy chair was positioned on the dais, and Faith assumed it was to provide a homey fireside chat kind of atmosphere.

Satisfied, she sat down at her desk and consulted her notes.

A few minutes later, Marlene strode into the room and approached Faith's desk, clipboard in hand. "Good. You're here." She checked her watch—a thin, black-banded affair with glittery rhinestones around its face. The kind of watch few women her age wore anymore. "Is everything ready? Guests will be arriving soon."

"I believe we're all set," Faith replied.

Marlene glanced at the yellow flowers, not yet placed in water. "Pretty," she noted, promptly returning her attention to the library door.

"They're daffodils or maybe jonquils. I'm not sure which is which."

"Daffodils," Marlene said matter-of-factly. "One stem, one flower. Small yellow jonquils—officially called *Narcissus jonquilla*—belong to the same plant family as daffodils, but they produce multiple small flowers on a single stem instead of a single large flower. Like those."

"I see," Faith said, genuinely impressed. "So, how was dinner? Did Brooke prepare her down-home country meal in honor of Hannibal, Missouri, and other points south?"

"We had panfried chicken, black-eyed peas, greens, mashed potatoes, and corn pone. And shoofly pie for dessert," Marlene reported. "Of course, for Mr. Ames she made something special. I personally took the tray up to his suite."

"I'm sorry I missed it," Faith said. "It sounds delicious."

"I sincerely hope he keeps that cat of his locked up for the evening," the assistant manager added. She scanned the room, no doubt searching for Watson. "Shall we—"

"I wonder if you might help me," someone interrupted.

At the sound of the voice, Faith turned to the door.

A tall woman who appeared well past the age of retirement approached them. She was impeccably dressed in a silk shantung suit, and her platinum hair was so perfect it might have been a wig. Snuggled under her arm was a white toy poodle. Walking next to the woman was a tall, distinguished-looking man wearing a tailored black suit.

"I understand you're the manager here," the woman said to Marlene.

Before Marlene could correct the assumption, the woman continued, "I seem to have misplaced my purse hook, and I wonder if someone might have turned it in."

"Purse hook?" Marlene repeated.

The woman held up a designer handbag in a color that matched her outfit exactly. "I'm talking about one of those hooks that holds your purse in place while you sit at a table."

"Oh yes," Marlene said. "I mean, I know what you're talking about, but no, I haven't heard that one has been turned in."

"It's not terribly expensive, though it does have some lovely rhinestones in it. I should very much like to find it." She raised flawlessly drawn sable brows. "I had it with me at dinner, but when I got up to leave the table, it was gone."

Marlene made suitable sounds of commiseration. "I'll ask the staff to search the manor for it. What is your name?"

"Constance Amboy." She motioned to the man next to her. "This is my husband, William." She patted the dog's head. "And this is our little darling Buffy."

Marlene jotted down a note on her clipboard. "There's a lost and found at the front desk. And you might also want to check the coffee and gift shop. Iris Alden, the manager, may have seen it. Sometimes people turn in things to her."

"You're very kind. And I do thank you," Constance said. Then she and William left.

Marlene sighed. "That's the second missing item I've been asked about today."

"What was the other one?" Faith asked.

"Callie Jones has misplaced a pen—one of those fancy jeweled varieties. You'd think these folks could keep track of their own belongings." She nodded at Faith to signal that their conversation was over.

Faith glanced at the door to see Mark Twain, aka Declan Ames, arriving with Edna. The infamous Faja was nowhere in sight.

As Marlene went to direct the pair to the places reserved for them, Faith sat down at her desk. Something niggled at the back of her mind. Two missing items in the short time this group of guests had been in residence? Faith frowned. She had almost been a third to report a lost item.

Faith opened the lower left drawer where her paperweight had turned up last night. She turned it over slowly in her hand, admiring its elegant simplicity, the tiny gold flowers surrounding the sepia image of her grandmother.

She never moved the paperweight from the corner of her desk. Well, not that she could remember, but she must have, for here it was. Of course, the newest member of the housekeeping staff might have put it in her drawer, fearful of knocking it off her desk.

But there was no more time to think about paperweights or purse hooks or whatever else had gone missing. The attendees were entering the library and taking their seats.

Faith went to join them, choosing a chair near the back of the group and behind a tall couple. She realized it was William and Constance Amboy.

On her left was a handsome man in his forties with spiky black hair. His deep-set brown eyes gave him a look of intrigue. He was well-groomed and sported the deliberate five-o'clock shadow that had become trendy.

The man gave her a boyish grin. "I've been looking forward to this performance ever since I heard about it. But I'm sure it's going to be a challenge for him to pull off."

"I'm certain Mr. Ames will provide a compelling program this evening," Faith replied. She hoped Declan's presentation drew raves, and she decided to change the subject in case the man started to critique the other guests. "I'm Faith Newberry, the librarian here."

"It's nice to meet you," he said, offering his hand. "Eric McCandless."

Faith shook his hand. "I hope you're enjoying the retreat so far."

"It's been great," Eric said enthusiastically. "My creative-writing instructor encouraged me to attend. He told me it would be helpful to my career." He smiled. "Not to brag or anything, but I like to think my style is similar to Twain's—you know, lots of adventure and forthright dialogue."

"Good luck with your writing," Faith said. She was pleased to meet such an eager writer with a good sense of humor.

"Thank you," Eric said. "It's a tough business, so I definitely need it."

She turned to study the actor, who was about to address the guests.

Edna had done a shockingly good job on Declan's makeup and hair, which she had obviously powdered carefully. He resembled the elder Twain, but he was more heavily mustached and white browed. Maybe Edna had done too much, for Declan had a pasty pallor, making his eyes look like black marbles by contrast. His white suit had been treated to appear old, like people were used to seeing in pictures of the great author. Of course, he wore a high collar and an oversize bow tie.

Faith fidgeted in her chair. That sense of dread she'd felt earlier had grown stronger. Perhaps it was just the worry about Declan and Clement not behaving themselves and causing a scene in front of the guests.

Professor George had changed from the denim shirt and jeans he'd been wearing while currying his horse. But he still looked every bit the cowboy in a shirt with a string tie, pants, boots, and a tweed jacket with ornamental piping. He took a place near the front and seemed as though he'd rather be anywhere else.

Just as Marlene took the podium and opened the session, the Morrissey sisters entered, Madeline appearing bright-eyed and eager and Corinna close at her sister's side, gaze roaming, then settling on Madeline.

Faith wondered if these two women were joined at the hip.

Marlene welcomed the guests, gave some suitable comments

related to the day's activity—trusting that they had enjoyed the nineteenth-century fashion show and that the special Southern cuisine served at dinner had been to their liking. Never at home with public speaking, the assistant manager seemed more than a little relieved to turn things over to Edna.

Edna rose. She looked like a consummate professional in a dark suit with pinstripes so thin they were almost invisible and a white blouse with cuffs that fell below the sleeves of her jacket. She wore no feminine adornments—not even a stud in her ear. Her sleek black hair draped the other ear in a fashionable cut.

Faith was surprised to see Edna without the thick-rimmed glasses, which made her piercing blue-gray eyes resemble a storm at sea. Her lips were thin and painted a dark red that contrasted with the whiteness of her skin.

Edna gripped both sides of the small podium and gave a taut smile that didn't quite reach her eyes. "Mark Twain was born Samuel Langhorne Clemens on November 30, 1835, in Florida, Missouri. He died on April 21, 1910, in Redding, Connecticut. He was a humorist, journalist, lecturer, and novelist, and he achieved worldwide notoriety for his travel narratives. You may be familiar with *The Innocents Abroad*, *Roughing It*, and *Life on the Mississippi*."

Edna's voice was well modulated but cold. Maybe she'd given this speech so many times that it had lost its verve.

"You may, however, be more familiar with his classic novels *The Adventures of Tom Sawyer* and *Adventures of Huckleberry Finn*," Edna went on. "Twain wrote an impressive and significant body of work, and he firmly established himself as one of America's best and most beloved writers," she concluded, then glanced at Declan.

The actor's head was bent, and he slouched in his chair, maybe to make himself seem older. Faith could see him only in profile, but he appeared to be sweating. He pulled a handkerchief from his pocket and dabbed at his face.

"And now," Edna said evenly, "I give you the celebrated Mark Twain."

Declan got to his feet. The white jacket hung awkwardly on his thin frame as he slowly shuffled to the easy chair on the raised dais.

Applause erupted from the eager audience.

Declan sat down but said nothing immediately. He shook his bushy white head, then replaced the handkerchief in the pocket of his suit and adjusted his bow tie. "'I have been complimented many times, and they always embarrass me,'" he said, affecting an ironic grin. "'I always feel that they have not said enough.'"

The spectators seemed to recognize Twain's famous quote and laughed as they were meant to do.

Declan waited for the laughter to cease. Then he leaned forward and straightened his shoulders. "'You don't know about me,'" he said in a younger voice and a completely different vernacular, "'without you have read a book by the name of *The Adventures of Tom Sawyer*; but that ain't no matter. That book was made by Mr. Mark Twain, and he told the truth, mainly. There was things which he stretched, but mainly he told the truth.'"

Faith realized that Declan was lifting lines from *Adventures of Huckleberry Finn*, and she thought he was doing it surprisingly well.

"'We catched fish, and talked, and we took a swim now and then to keep off sleepiness,'" he continued. "'It was kind of solemn, drifting down the big still river, laying on our backs looking up at the stars, and we didn't ever feel like talking loud, and it warn't often that we laughed, only a kind of a low chuckle.'"

The applause of the group partly covered Declan's raspy intake of breath. Faith had been watching Declan very closely, and she'd heard it. Surely that was not intended to mimic the voice of Huck.

But the actor seemed to recover and straightened his shoulders once more. "'We had mighty good weather, as a general thing, and nothing ever happened to us at all, that night, nor the next, nor the next.'"

The crowd listened with rapt attention.

"'We said there warn't no home like a raft, after all,'" Declan went on. "'Other places do seem so cramped up and smothery, but a raft don't. You feel mighty free and easy and comfortable on a raft.'"

Declan's breathlessness grew more pronounced. After a moment, he rubbed a hand across his jaw as elderly men tend to do.

And suddenly Huckleberry Finn was gone. The boy became a man with doddery movements and a voice punctuated by breathy pauses. "'I was sorry to have my name mentioned as one of the great authors, because they have a sad habit of dying off. Chaucer is dead, Spencer is dead, so is Milton, so is Shakespeare, and I'm not feeling so well myself.'"

Faith recognized Twain's quote, but what had her holding her breath was the fact that Declan had started slurring his words. She scooted forward in her chair as the actor's face blanched even under the makeup. Indeed, he did not look well at all.

Edna rushed to Declan's side. She said something to him and moved in front of him, blocking the view of the audience.

Marlene pressed toward Declan and Edna, her face a mask of shock and confusion. "Are you all right, Mr. Ames?" she asked, kneeling.

As one, the group of guests leaned in, some standing as they strained to hear what was going on.

Faith heard a dull thump, the sound of something—or someone—falling to the floor. Edna and Marlene still blocked the view of the platform, so Faith jumped up from her chair, her heart pounding, and tried to make out what was going on.

Marlene rose from her knees and craned her neck to see into the crowd.

Faith glimpsed Declan through the gap. He was no longer upright in his chair.

"Call 911!" Marlene hollered. "Mr. Ames has collapsed."

6

Faith ran to the front of the library. She arrived just in time to see Edna pressing Declan's carotid artery and Marlene feeling his wrists.

The two women exchanged one brief but horrified glance. A glance that said there would be no more stories from the still, blue lips of Declan Ames.

Faith felt too stunned to move. She looked around and noticed Wolfe entering the library.

Leaving the door open, Wolfe rushed toward the little group on the platform, cell phone in hand. His face was grim as he reported the emergency.

He disconnected and turned to the audience. "The program is over," he called out. "Please clear this room immediately and return to your rooms."

Faith helped to steer the shocked guests from the library, telling them the ambulance was coming and that the best thing they could do was cooperate.

Most of the guests left immediately, but a few stayed behind. They exclaimed to one another, obviously eager to see what was going on. Some stood in stricken silence, gawking at the scene.

"Please, you must leave now," Faith said to the Morrissey sisters, who lingered at the door.

The usually effervescent Madeline seemed traumatized. Her hands flew to her cheeks. "Oh no!" she cried. "I never wanted that to happen."

Faith turned to Corinna, hoping she could get her sister moving.

The woman stood perfectly still, head high, shoulders rigid in her tweed suit jacket. Her features were fixed in what Faith could only describe as a look of satisfaction.

But there was no time to think about the strange reactions of the Morrissey sisters. Faith continued ushering everyone out of the library and into the hallway as sirens whined and came closer and closer.

Brooke sprinted down the hall, anxiety wreathing her pretty features. "Where's everyone going? What's happened?" she asked breathlessly, blue eyes wide with fright.

"It's awful," Faith said. "One minute we were all wrapped up in the *Adventures of Huckleberry Finn* and then—"

"What are you talking about?"

"It's Mr. Ames. The actor portraying Mark Twain for our guests."

"What about him?" Brooke asked, her face drained of color.

"He collapsed," Faith responded. She took a deep breath as she recalled the horrified glance Marlene and Edna had exchanged. "And he looks dead."

Brooke grabbed Faith's hand, clinging to her like someone drowning. Brooke wasn't a weakling, but she was tenderhearted and couldn't bear to see anyone—human or animal—suffer.

"I don't know anything for sure. Maybe he'll be okay," Faith said, unnerved by Brooke's strong reaction.

Brooke released Faith's hand and averted her face.

"The paramedics are here. I've got to show them where to go." Faith hurried to meet them.

The emergency medical technicians followed wordlessly with their equipment and foreboding gurney as Faith led them to the library. She held the doors open and watched them do what they were trained to do. Though Lighthouse Bay was a small town, it had its share of sudden illness, injury, and calamity at sea.

For her part, Faith never heard a siren without whispering a prayer for the person whose emergency had summoned it.

She stood several feet away, giving the technicians room, and prayed for Declan.

Marlene had taken Edna aside, supporting her with an arm around her. The visibly distraught woman was weeping copious tears.

Officer Bryan Laddy rushed into the library. He seemed to take in the entire scene in a flash.

"What's happened here?" a deep voice behind her broke in.

Faith turned to see Andy Garris. The tall police chief who had kept the peace in Lighthouse Bay for years was a calming presence during this disturbing time.

Garris reminded Faith of her father, a retired Springfield, Massachusetts, police sergeant. Martin Newberry was tall with a kind and generous heart, despite having frequently rubbed elbows with people who weren't exactly model citizens. The same could be said for the chief.

"His name is Declan Ames," Faith answered. "He's a guest at the manor and an actor. He was portraying Mark Twain, but he collapsed during the performance." She shook her head. "It was awful, happening right here with an audience watching. And poor Miss Grimmell."

Chief Garris searched her face, then took a few steps forward. Faith followed. Quietly, they waited as the EMTs worked and Officer Laddy spoke with Marlene and Edna.

Declan was being placed onto the gurney. Behind the makeup and powdered hair, his face was a ghostly gray, and he wasn't moving at all.

Wolfe approached the chief, his features grave. "They'll transport him to the hospital, but there's no heartbeat. They believe he passed away seconds after his collapse. We understand he is a heart patient and he had a heart attack last year."

The chief lowered his head as though in tribute to the fallen man. Then he nodded at Wolfe. "I'll need to talk with those who were around him tonight and with anyone who knows him." He spoke steadily and with authority, but compassion tinged his blue eyes.

"Of course," Wolfe replied.

"But that can wait until tomorrow. Are there any relatives we should notify?" Garris motioned to Edna, who followed the inert Declan and the emergency personnel to a rear exit.

"Miss Grimmell is Mr. Ames's assistant and publicist," Wolfe said. "She says both of his parents are dead, but he has a younger brother living somewhere around Boston. According to Miss Grimmell, there has been no contact between the two for years."

"Did you find out anything else?" the chief asked.

"Declan Ames is a stage name, and his real name is Declan Kilpatrick," Wolfe said. "Apparently, he's been estranged from his family for a long time."

"Sorry about all this," Garris said. "We'll follow up on the brother and hold on to the personal effects of Mr. Kilpatrick until we've checked things out."

Faith had noticed Officer Laddy withdraw some items from Declan's pockets and place them in a plastic bag. A wallet, keys, and some papers. Perhaps they were his notes from the evening's performance, though Faith hadn't seen him use notes. His rhetoric had seemed to flow from memory, at least until he became breathless and started to slur his words.

"It would be best to keep the suite he was staying in sealed from outsiders," the chief continued.

Wolfe nodded.

Laddy joined them, and Faith and Wolfe walked the police officers to the door. No doubt guests would be watching from the loggia until the official vehicles drove away. Their curiosity was only natural, but at least they weren't bombarding them with questions. Most had obediently gone to their rooms.

Faith scanned the area for Brooke, but there was no sign of her. She'd hated having to leave her, knowing how surprisingly upset she was. When she'd returned to the library with the EMTs, Brooke was already gone.

Now as they passed the Great Hall Gallery, Faith spotted Clement leaning against the statue of Dame Agatha Christie the way a cowboy might relax against a fence post. She almost expected to see a blade of grass between his teeth.

Clement gazed out the window, but Faith was too far away to read his expression. Clement and Declan knew each other, perhaps were colleagues, since both were members of the same historical society, but they were definitely not friends. Declan had decried Clement's biography as unworthy of the paper it was written on. She shuddered. What was Clement thinking at this moment?

Grave illness or death always changed a person, sometimes in positive ways and sometimes feeding an intrinsic bitterness. What had Madeline meant with her shocked exclamation? What had Corinna been thinking when she stood at the back of the library with that look of conquest?

"I'll come back tomorrow," Chief Garris said to Wolfe as he zipped his jacket. "Without the black-and-white."

Faith appreciated how the chief tried to shield the manor's guests from an unnecessary invasion of privacy or reminders of the awful scene they had witnessed.

"Thank you," Wolfe said, shaking the policeman's hand.

Faith and Wolfe stood watching as Chief Garris and Officer Laddy climbed into their cars and drove away. Neither moved to close the door. Instead, they allowed the brisk April air to waft over them.

It was late, and only a thumbnail moon mitigated the dark skies. The manor's impeccably manicured grounds with its blossoming magnolias and spiraling firs stretched out before them in a panorama of order and serenity. But tonight, chaos had erupted. A man had died.

"Are you all right?" Wolfe asked after a long moment.

"Yes, but it's just so . . ." Faith trailed off, not knowing how to express what she was feeling. She hadn't liked Declan from the first moment they met, but now he was gone.

"You've had a long day and a tough experience," he said gently. "I'll walk you home."

She almost breathed a sigh of relief at the offer. There was something so strong and serene about Wolfe that made her feel safe. His mere presence was comforting.

"Come on," he said, taking her arm lightly. "I'm not letting you go back to the cottage alone."

As they walked slowly away from the manor, Faith said, "You didn't know Declan Ames—or Kilpatrick, did you?" Wolfe had said as much in an earlier conversation, but she needed to talk about the man and what had happened. How could she think of anything else?

"No. I understand from Marlene that he hasn't been on the touring circuit very long, but he had already made quite an impression, particularly in Missouri and Indiana. I wanted to hear his entire presentation, but I arrived late. I didn't want to interrupt, so I went to the second floor to listen. He had just started in on the Huck Finn story, and I must say I was hooked. His Missouri backwoods accent was quite impressive."

"So that's how you got there so quickly after it happened," Faith said. "You were up in the balcony."

Wolfe nodded. "When Declan started slurring his speech, I leaned over to get a better look. And then I heard the thump and saw him on the floor." He sighed. "He was too young. Much too young."

It's enough to give anyone pause, Faith thought. "He wasn't completely an unknown among the group," she said. "Some of our other guests were part of the same historical society in Hartford. Bergen something."

"Yes, I've heard of it."

"They weren't exactly fans of his," Faith said, chewing the inside of her cheek as she recalled the awkward scene with Clement. "Professor

Clement George is a historian, and he's writing a new biography of Bret Harte. Declan was positively rude to him." She felt oddly guilty about speaking ill of the dead.

Wolfe drew in his breath and was quiet for a long moment as they continued toward Faith's cottage. "That must have been awkward. I'm surprised that Declan would behave like that."

"It was definitely awkward," Faith admitted.

"So who are the other guests in the historical society?" Wolfe asked.

"Corinna and Madeline Morrissey."

"Have you met Dr. Morrissey and her sister?"

"Dr. Morrissey?" Faith echoed.

"Yes, Madeline is known to have her eccentricities, but she's a brilliant historian. She's lectured in colleges and universities all over the world."

"Madeline?" Faith repeated, stunned. "The one with the Christmas morning look who chats on a mile a minute like a precocious child?"

"That's the one," Wolfe said. "But her stone-faced sister keeps her on an even keel. She's quite the protector, undoubtedly the one who keeps Madeline's antics and most flamboyant comments out of the papers."

"I had no idea," Faith said. "I could see Corinna as a professor or a doctor but not Madeline."

"They come from Falmouth," he continued. "Most of the locals know them, though they spend most of their time buried deep in academia in Boston."

Faith recalled her first conversation with them, then Madeline's reaction when she had urged the sisters out of the library after Declan collapsed. Madeline had been visibly shaken. *Oh no. I never wanted that to happen*, she had said.

Never wanted what to happen? To see Declan dead? Faith shook herself. *I'm being melodramatic. It was probably nothing at all.* And yet, it was Corinna's face—that terrible look of avenged satisfaction—that unnerved her still.

"We have some real literati at this retreat," Wolfe said. "In defense of Mr. Mark Twain, aka Declan Ames, aka Declan Kilpatrick, maybe they're all too hard on the actor."

"I'm not sure there was any love lost between him and his assistant either," Faith said. She'd been sobbing at Declan's side after his collapse, but when he had reprimanded her in front of everyone, she'd seemed angry, her face blossoming red.

Wolfe stopped on the path and turned to her. "Are you questioning if Declan died of natural causes?"

"No. We were all there. We saw him collapse. I'm just saying that if it was something other than a heart attack, we wouldn't have to look far for suspects."

"The chief will order an autopsy. When someone dies suddenly like that, I believe that's the standard procedure," he said. Then he smiled down at her, his blue eyes mischievous but tender. "But I think you've been reading too many mysteries. Not that we haven't had our share of mysteries around here."

"Don't remind me," she teased.

His expression turned serious. "Our task now is to get through this retreat and keep the guests distracted from what's happened."

They reached her cottage door.

Faith opened it with her key and turned to Wolfe. "Thanks for walking me home."

"It was my pleasure."

"I'm glad you weren't off in Paris or London or someplace." She laughed to lighten her words, to make it seem that she wasn't over the moon that he was back at the manor and taking charge of things.

Watson leaped down from the couch as soon as the door opened and began twining around Faith's legs, mewling a welcome.

Wolfe stooped to stroke the black fur. "Take care of her," he said to the cat.

Watson immediately began to purr.

"No Edgar Allan Poe for you tonight," Wolfe told Faith. "Nothing heavier than Jane Austen."

7

Faith had slept well, despite the wrenching events of the previous night.

Thanks to her wise grandmother, she had learned to "Have courage for the great sorrows of life and patience for the small ones; and when you have laboriously accomplished your daily task, go to sleep in peace. God is awake." The maxim by Victor Hugo was one worth living by.

Still, as she and Watson walked to the manor the next morning, the birds seemed a little less jubilant, the sky a shade more somber. She hoped the guests had been able to rest despite the dreadful event of the night before, but it could hardly help but cast a gloom over the rest of the retreat.

When Faith opened the door at the manor, Watson raced inside and disappeared.

"Be good, Rumpy," she called after him, even though she knew he didn't hear her.

Rather than head directly for the library, Faith went to the dining room, where the guests were gathered for breakfast. The room was full. The attendees' curiosity evidently overruled any temptation to sleep in and skip the morning meal. She sat down at an empty table.

It wasn't long before Wolfe moved to the front and addressed the crowd. "We regret to announce that Mr. Declan Ames, the Mark Twain impressionist, has died of an apparent heart attack last evening."

Several people gasped.

"The authorities are working to notify family members and to make fitting arrangements," Wolfe went on. "The retreat will continue as planned, and the Castleton Manor staff is at your disposal for any needs you might have. We extend our deep condolences to Mr. Ames's family and friends and to Miss Edna Grimmell, Mr. Ames's faithful assistant and publicist, whose privacy we know you will respect." He left the room before anyone could ask questions.

Faith knew there was no point for Wolfe to linger after the announcement. There was little else he could tell them until the investigation uncovered facts pertaining to the case.

He was followed out by Marlene, who had left in the ambulance with Edna and most likely had seen her to her suite for the night.

What was going through Edna's mind as she woke to a new day? And what, Faith suddenly thought, was to be done about Declan's Ragdoll? Edna was allergic to Faja, and she was obviously not fond of the cat because she had referred to her as "mangy" and a "fool animal."

Faith stopped by the coffee and gift shop, a feature of the manor many guests enjoyed. She found Iris Alden, the shop manager, and Marlene engaged in conversation.

However late her night had been, Marlene didn't look any worse for wear—makeup flawlessly applied, her hair neatly arranged. Small green gems in her ears matched her forest-green dress. She was leaning forward, her hands folded on top of a clipboard resting on the counter. She wore a serious expression, which was nothing new for Marlene.

"Good morning," Iris said to Faith, sounding more than a little grateful for the interruption.

Iris was a retired museum conservator who specialized in Early American decorative art. When she and her husband, a former professor of German literature, retired to Lighthouse Bay, Iris realized she didn't want to stay retired, so she had taken over the management of the manor's coffee and gift shop.

Faith returned the greeting, noting that at least this morning Marlene was not rearranging Iris's displays. It was the only thing about Iris's job that she clearly did not appreciate. In her gracious way, Iris managed to endure the micromanagement. "And good morning to you too, Marlene. I thought you might allow yourself to sleep in after your very long night." As soon as she said the words, she regretted them. She was well aware that Marlene never slept in.

"Unfortunately," Marlene said, a bit wearily but not without her usual irony, "duty calls."

"Would you like a cup of coffee?" Iris asked Faith.

"Yes, that would be wonderful," she answered.

"Coming right up." Iris went over to the coffeepot and poured a tall cup. She handed it to Faith with a smile.

"Thank you," Faith said as she inhaled the rich aroma.

Marlene tapped the clipboard on the counter in front of her. "Mrs. Amboy's purse hook and Mrs. Jones's gold designer pen that were reported missing yesterday haven't turned up in lost and found yet. I was just asking Iris if she'd seen them."

Iris shook her head. "But it's rather early in the retreat, isn't it?" She looked down, straightening a small display of colorful magnets on the counter. "I was so sorry to hear about Mr. Ames," she continued softly.

It struck Faith as ironic to be discussing lost-and-found objects in the same conversation as untimely death.

"Yes," Marlene said, straightening her shoulders. "But we will all do our best to keep things going in a normal fashion." It was as much a directive as a statement of confidence.

Faith caught Iris's knowing look.

They all turned at the sound of the door opening, ushering in Edna. The woman's turbulent sea-gray eyes seemed magnified behind her large glasses, and the lines in her forehead puckered. Faith wondered if they were signs of stress or grief.

"I've been searching for you, Ms. Russell," Edna said. She had been visibly distraught last night, but today Declan's assistant and publicist spoke in a steady voice. Faith marveled at the woman's control.

"How can I be of assistance?" Marlene asked.

"I shall require a key to Mr. Ames's suite because I will need to tend to Faja." At the mention of the Ragdoll cat, Edna's thin crimson lips turned down slightly. "I intend to leave as soon as Mr. Ames is released." She lowered her head as if in private mourning. "But I will see to the animal."

See to the animal? Faith repeated silently. Was Edna offering to care for the cat she clearly did not like? Or did she view Faja's care as a matter of duty—a salute to the dead man?

Marlene folded her arms and regarded Edna. It was a pose that had the power to intimidate. Still, Marlene's response was kind and measured. "We are so sorry for your loss, and we understand your wish to get away as soon as possible, but it may be some time before . . ." She seemed hesitant to say what had to be said. "That is, it may take a few days before his body is released. Next of kin must be notified, and we need to await the results of the autopsy."

Edna cleared her throat. "I've been the one to see to his affairs. There's no one else to handle things except me. You can bet that so-called brother of his won't lift a finger."

"I understand," Marlene said, not unsympathetically. "Now, as for a key to the suite, I'm afraid that would be against our policy. Besides, the police might need to search the room for Mr. Ames's personal items and to confirm the cause of his death."

Edna swept back the hair that draped the left side of her face. "But what about Faja?" she asked.

Why this show of concern for the cat? Was Edna willing to sacrifice for the sake of her departed boss, or might she have another reason to get inside his suite? Was there something in there that she didn't want anyone to see? Faith shook her head. Her imagination was getting the best of her.

"It's most kind of you to offer to take care of the animal," Marlene said. "We can bring the cat to you, and she can stay with you in your suite."

Faith could see Edna's nose twitching just talking about the Ragdoll. She wondered if any moment a sneeze might erupt.

"I have handled Faja's care when I was needed but always at Declan's lodging," Edna explained. "Couldn't we keep it that way? He was very fond of her, and he wouldn't want just anyone to look after her. But unfortunately, I am allergic to cats."

Marlene narrowed her eyes, clearly not understanding Edna's reticence.

"Perhaps you might be more comfortable leaving Faja at the kennels," Faith suggested to Edna. "She'd be well cared for, and you could check in on her anytime to make sure she's all right." *Unlikely*, Faith thought, given Edna's obvious antipathy to the cat.

Marlene looked like she was about to object to the idea. After all, the decision would be hers or Wolfe's, not Faith's. "Well," she said slowly, "that might be a suitable arrangement until we know the disposition of Mr. Ames's belongings."

"Surely that won't take long," Edna said. She crossed her arms and clutched the elbows of her jersey knit dress, which matched the color of her eyes. The shade reminded Faith of bruised clouds before a thunderstorm.

"I'll see that one of our staff members picks up Faja this morning," Marlene said firmly. "She'll be quite safe and cared for at the kennels." She took a few steps to one side. "Is there anything else we can do to assist you?"

Edna's gaze darted from Faith to Iris and back to Marlene. She shook back the offending swatch of hair that had fallen over her eye.

Faith waited, watching Edna. Despite the woman's grimness, Edna was an attractive woman. Faith couldn't help but wonder if Edna had harbored some romantic feelings for her employer.

After a lengthy, uncomfortable silence, Edna said in clipped, proprietary tones, "I would like to be informed the moment there is any news." With that, she spun on her heel and marched out of the gift shop.

Marlene picked up her clipboard and left with a weary sigh.

Iris raised her eyebrows. "That was interesting," she remarked.

"It certainly was," Faith agreed. "Thanks for the coffee. I need to get going too. I want to touch base with Brooke before her day gets too hectic. We haven't had a minute to talk with all that's been happening. The guests are keeping us busy."

"I know how that is," Iris said.

Faith grinned. "Look on the bright side: Marlene didn't touch any of your displays." She patted Iris's arm. "They're beautiful, by the way."

"Thank you," Iris said.

Faith walked out of the shop and went downstairs. She had just started down the corridor toward the kitchen when she nearly bumped into Laura, who was carrying a large box.

"Let me give you a hand," Faith said, reaching out to help steady the load. "What's in here? The crown jewels?"

Laura laughed. "New dessert dishes I'm taking up to the dining room."

They set the box on a table someone had wisely placed next to the elevator.

"Brooke is making a special custard and wants to serve it in these crystal dishes," Laura continued. "You know what a perfectionist she is about presentation."

"Yes, I know." Faith thought about the previous night and how upset Brooke had been. She searched Laura's light-blue eyes. "Is she all right?"

"I think so. But the news is so awful." Laura coiled a strand of blonde hair behind a slightly protruding ear.

"It is," Faith said softly. "Sadly, Mr. Ames had a bad heart."

Laura shot Faith a guarded look. "At least now he won't be coming around and bothering Brooke anymore."

Faith studied the waifish young woman's face. "Mr. Ames was bothering Brooke?"

"She was upset. I could tell by the way she was talking to that actor." Laura lowered her head as though ashamed of sounding disrespectful.

"I didn't hear what they said, and they didn't know I was there. I had come in early to help because Brooke's been . . . well, you know—"

Faith nodded. Brooke had been behaving strangely the last couple of days. Maybe Declan had come in to talk about his special diet. Maybe something wasn't to his liking and he had been rude and uncomplimentary, as he had been with Clement.

"I'll go cheer her up," Faith said, patting Laura's arm. "Are you sure you can handle that box?"

Laura raised a skinny arm and flexed her muscle with a laugh. "Nothing to it," she said as she picked up the box and stepped into the elevator.

Faith continued down the corridor to the kitchen, prepared to walk on eggshells.

Brooke stood at the counter, reading a cookbook. She glanced up when Faith walked in. "Come here and look at this fantastic recipe. It's for a special custard made with cream cheese and caramel—Bavarian, I think."

Faith walked over to the counter.

Brooke moved over a little so Faith could see the cookbook. "Read those rich ingredients. What do you think?"

Faith tried to rally from her initial surprise. Here was not the distracted, brooding Brooke but the friend she knew and loved. She wore a sparkling-white chef's coat over a silk blouse of some gorgeous shade of blue. Studying Brooke's averted face, however, Faith thought she glimpsed shadows beneath her friend's eyes that her makeup had not entirely concealed.

Brooke pointed a blue-polished nail to a page in the book. "And I thought I'd add cinnamon and just a touch of cardamom to round it out."

"Yes, it sounds delicious," Faith agreed, elated by Brooke's return to her usual enthusiasm but puzzled by the turnaround. "I'm sure everyone will love it." She paused, straightening. "I saw Laura at the elevator taking up the crystal dessert dishes. They'll be perfect for such an elegant concoction."

"I think so too. Would you like a cup of coffee?" Brooke asked, already heading for the coffeepot. She whirled around, the skirt of her dress flaring under the chef's coat. "And there are blueberry scones if you want them."

Faith raised her cup. "I already grabbed coffee." She took a seat at the small table in the corner. "But I'll have a scone if you'll join me."

Brooke said nothing at first, busying herself filling a cup and placing scones on two small plates. "For a few minutes," she mumbled. "Tons to do today. Shrimp and crab salad are on the menu for lunch, and that takes a lot of prep time."

"It sounds great, and I'm sure the guests will love it."

"What are the guests doing today?" Brooke asked.

"Professor Jennings from Plymouth will soon be presenting an all-day seminar on nineteenth-century American poets," Faith answered. "I've heard him speak once or twice, and he knows how to keep his listeners totally engaged."

"I was always partial to Emily Dickinson," Brooke mused as she put the plates and her cup of coffee on a tray. "There's something so homey about her poems. Well, the ones I can understand anyway. She wrote about everyday things in the most heavenly ways."

"She certainly did."

"When I was in high school, I had to recite the one about how the sun rises. Something about a ribbon . . ." Brooke set the tray in front of Faith and sat down next to her.

"'A ribbon at a time,'" Faith supplied as she took a sip of coffee.

Brooke followed suit, and they sat silently for a long moment.

"You seem bright-eyed and bushy-tailed this morning," Faith said lightly. A surreptitious glance to her left revealed the shadows under Brooke's eyes. Seeing them close up, Faith knew she hadn't imagined them.

Brooke motioned to Faith's plate of scones. "Have one," she urged, adding no comment to Faith's observation.

"You don't have to ask me twice," Faith joked. She picked up one of the scones and took a bite. "Delicious."

"By the way, Diva is full of vinegar today," Brooke said. "And Bling keeps circling the aquarium and chasing her like mad. They're both like a couple of kids playing ring-around-the-rosy."

"That's wonderful news. It sounds like Diva has fully recovered."

"Where's Watson today?" Brooke asked, then took a bite of a scone.

"Oh, he's around here somewhere." Faith smiled. "You know him. He pops up at the most surprising moments when you have no idea he's even in the neighborhood."

Silence descended again.

They were both dancing around the events of the previous night. Faith had had to leave Brooke in the hallway, dazed and uncomprehending. When she'd returned with the EMTs, Brooke was already gone. Perhaps she'd had the night to recover from the awfulness of learning someone had passed away right here at the manor.

Brooke suddenly turned to face her directly. "Are you all right?" she asked softly. "I mean, after what happened last night?"

It was the question Faith had wanted to ask her, but Brooke had turned the tables.

"It was awful. No one could have predicted it or done anything." Faith waited for Brooke to say something. When she didn't reply, Faith added, "Wherever he is now, I hope he's at peace."

When silence once again descended, Faith glanced at Brooke, who was staring straight ahead, her expression unreadable.

Brooke stood up abruptly. "Well, that salad isn't going to make itself." She gave Faith a quick hug and hurried over to the counter.

Faith stared after her in wonder. She wanted to follow and press her about what Laura had said, but the insistent jangle of her cell phone broke in. It was Marlene.

"I need your assistance," Marlene said without preamble. "Come to my office, please." She disconnected before Faith could respond, which undoubtedly meant that later wasn't an option.

8

"There you are," Marlene said. She stood at her desk, frowning, hands perched on her hips.

Faith was taken aback. It had been less than two minutes since she received the call. Then she realized that Marlene's glare most likely had more to do with the fact that Watson, who had appeared out of nowhere, was scooting inside the assistant manager's office ahead of her.

"Oh, sorry," Faith said, scooping up Watson in her arms. "Where did you come from?" she scolded the cat gently.

Watson made no response. He seemed intent on teasing Marlene with his unwanted presence, though Faith had a suspicion that the cat was growing on her.

"I'd like you to take Mr. Ames's cat to the kennels this morning," Marlene said. "Annie is expecting you." She removed a key from her key ring on the desk and handed it to Faith. "Here's the key to the Mark Twain Suite. Return it promptly."

Faith held her tongue. So much for the work she was planning to get done in the library this morning. And Annie Jennings, the young kennel attendant, had no doubt been instructed to clear her calendar as well.

"Miss Grimmell is with Wolfe and Chief Garris," Marlene continued. "They're waiting for me to join them, so I'd appreciate it if you handle this right away." She gave Watson a disparaging glance before saying to Faith, "After all, you have a way with cats, don't you?"

"Of course," Faith said. "Come on, Watson. We have our orders."

Upstairs, guests were hurrying toward the highly theatrical music room, where the poetry seminar was being held.

Watson squirmed in her arms.

Faith set him down. "Behave yourself," she told the cat.

Watson didn't linger. He immediately scampered away.

Constance Amboy, dressed in an elegant royal-blue dress, strode across the foyer with her husband, William, whose white hair shone like sun-drenched snow.

Constance stopped when she noticed Faith and smiled broadly. "Oh, Miss Newberry, I wonder if you'd be good enough to let Ms. Russell know that I've found my purse hook."

"I'm glad to hear it," Faith said, "and I'll be sure to let her know."

"I must have dropped it. That charming Mr. McCandless said he found it on the floor in the dining room. I'm so happy to have it back." Constance patted her fashionable bag. "And I shall be much more careful with it from now on."

The housekeeping staff had been instructed to make a careful search the same evening Constance had reported the loss. It struck Faith as odd that they had missed the purse hook but Eric McCandless had found it.

"Oh, one more thing," Constance said. "Callie Jones has her gold pen back too. Wonderful, isn't it?"

"It certainly is," Faith said.

Constance and William walked away.

Faith was relieved that the missing items had been found. That was one less thing for Marlene to worry about. Clutching the key, she headed for the Mark Twain Suite.

Silence reigned in the carpeted hallway. With the guests attending the poetry seminar downstairs, there was no sound as she approached. She'd seen the Mark Twain Suite shortly after it had been redone and recalled its impressive decor. It would be nice to have another peek. Still, she dreaded putting the key in the lock. The man who had last inhabited this room—less than a day ago—was dead.

She pushed the door open warily and stepped inside. Beyond a small foyer, an expansive sitting room featured a leather sofa and a low coffee table. An overhead fan resembled a paddle wheel.

Or maybe, Faith thought, *I'm imagining myself on a riverboat with Mark Twain.*

She glanced around the suite. It was spotless, as though the housekeeping staff had recently cleaned it from top to bottom, and it seemed like no one had resided in it at all. There were no suitcases in sight, and she spotted nothing of a personal nature in the entire place. The only thing she noticed was a newspaper on the coffee table.

The modern bed, with its coverlet of brown and gold, was made up. It was a massive piece of furniture with a faux Venetian oak headboard, and she couldn't help comparing it with the one she'd seen in the author's Hartford home.

She turned away from the bed, aware again of intruding on a man's private domain. Not Twain's but that of Declan, whose ghost, if she believed in ghosts—which she didn't—seemed to hover.

She chided herself and continued with her errand.

It was then she heard something in the eerie quiet. It was a shuffling noise and then a soft mewling. Faja, of course.

She ducked around the corner, and there was the Ragdoll in a cage.

"Oh, you sweet thing," Faith said. "What are you doing in there?" The cage was ample, but Faith hated to see any animal confined. Even the kennels at the manor, though they were large and airy and often necessary, made her wince.

Why had Declan thought Faja needed to be caged in his own suite? Perhaps he worried that the cat, being in new surroundings, might sneak out and get lost. After all, the Ragdoll had gotten away from Edna and run into the library.

Faith lifted the latch, and Faja leaped out.

The cat bypassed a litter box and began sniffing around the suite, no doubt searching for something to eat.

But nothing resembling food was visible. Perhaps Declan had fed

Faja with table scraps and kept no kibble or tins of cat food in his room. She opened the refrigerator, but it contained nothing but gleaming white walls and empty wire racks.

Ragdolls were not known to be especially vocal, but they would remind you with a soft mewling when they were hungry. And Faja was hungry. Had Declan not fed his beloved cat before his performance?

Faja looked up expectantly at the human who just might work some magic. She had a distinct coat—lots of fluffy white fur and soft brown markings on her back and tail that darkened at the neck and head. The perfectly pointed ears were outlined in the brown hue of rich, dark coffee. Her stunning blue eyes were accentuated by the same deep color.

Faja mewed again softly, and Faith was smitten.

Grabbing the leash off the top of the cage, she picked up Faja and cradled her in her arms. "You're all hair and collar," Faith said. Instead of hooking the leash to the gaudy jeweled collar, she stuffed it into her pocket, anxious now to flee the overbearing suite.

In a flash, she knew that she wouldn't go directly to the kennels. She'd return the key to the Mark Twain Suite to Marlene and take Faja to her cottage to get something to eat.

The cat was snooping around the herb garden again, allowing himself a roll or two in the plot of catnip, when he spied his human heading for the cottage. He envisioned the soft couch by the window where the sun streamed in. It was midmorning, and he could use a nap.

But what was that? He hunkered down in the soft tangle of greenery and opened his eyes wide. Is that what I think it is? Is my person really carrying that hairy beast who tried to steal my dinner?

He stared at the animal, her bushy tail waving in the air. He was suspicious of cats who paraded their fat tails like banners in the wind. Who really needed them, anyway? He got along just fine with his handsome little stub. He supposed he had a full tail once, but it had been so long ago that he could barely remember. Still, he sometimes wished he had one to swish back and forth when he had the notion.

He watched them pass by his hiding place. Usually, he would run out and greet his human. After all, she was the one who fed him. And when he was afraid or tired, her lap was the coziest place he knew. Her distinctive voice carried softly on the wind, but she wasn't calling him. Instead, she was talking to the cat lying like a fuzzy blanket in her arms.

He crept out of the garden and stealthily followed them to the cottage. The door opened, and they went in—to his house! Like a flash, he zoomed inside too and flew under the couch. His human hadn't even noticed. He scooted farther under the couch and peeked through the narrow opening.

They approached his food bowl, but he wasn't alarmed. It was empty.

But then his human started scooping delicious nuggets from the magic bag that lived under the sink. She poured them right into his bowl. Was nothing sacred?

The cat watched the interloper scarf down the kibble and sniff around the kitchen. And then she followed his human into the living room, stopped at the rug by the fireplace, and plopped down on it.

Well, make yourself at home, why don't you?

And she did. Curling her bushy tail around herself, the feline began to purr. She didn't even move when his human put on her jacket and left the cottage.

The cat rested his head on his paws. He might as well catch forty winks while that little beast was sleeping.

When he woke up, he heard a familiar jingly sound. He peered through the darkness of the couch's underbelly.

The invader was up and padding around the living room, sniffing and batting his round, rolling toy across the floor.

First his dish, then his toy. This was a fine kettle of fish.

The ball hit his nose.

A hairy paw swiped back and forth in an attempt to reach under the couch.

He batted the toy back. Take that, you freeloader!

And she did. She whapped the ball back under the couch. Delicate paws reached, swept back and forth.

This was interesting. He batted the ball back, and this time it went clear into the kitchen.

When the furry feline came back, she whacked the ball faster and faster until once again it rolled smack into his nose.

He clutched it doglike in his mouth.

Two blue eyes appeared under the couch.

He peered back.

The cat sat on her hairy haunches, waiting.

Actually, this was rather fun. He flattened himself and crept forward to the front of the couch. He'd have a talk with this unwelcome visitor, at least to let her know who was boss. Soon he was facing the little invader, gripping the jingly ball tightly.

Envying her large tail, he had to admit she was rather pretty.

She lowered her head, a look of daring in her eyes.

Maybe it wasn't so bad having a playmate. Tentatively, he swatted the ball. Just try and get it before I do!

Faith hurried back to the manor after leaving Faja to explore her new surroundings. It wouldn't do to wait too long to inform Marlene that Declan's cat was at her cottage instead of the kennels.

"I took care of that little errand," Faith announced when she stepped inside the assistant manager's office.

"Fine," Marlene responded without glancing up from her desk.

Her furrowed brow and darting eyes meant she was troubled about something.

"But I just didn't have the heart to put her in the kennels," Faith said. "Not after finding her locked up in a cage in Declan's suite."

Marlene remained silent, obviously still distracted.

"The poor thing was hungry," Faith continued. "There wasn't a bit of cat food in the room. Why do you suppose Declan kept her in a cage?"

"Probably because she'd run off like she did before," Marlene said idly, her attention still on her desk.

"I phoned Annie and told her I would keep Faja at my cottage for the time being," Faith went on. "There's no reason why she can't have the run of the house. She's really a sweet cat."

"Hmm," Marlene mumbled. "Your Mr. Watson may eat her for supper, but I don't suppose it will matter to Miss Grimmell one way or the other."

"Well, I wanted to let you know."

Whatever lay on her desk had reclaimed Marlene's attention, and she barely looked up as Faith excused herself and left to return to her cottage for lunch.

When she turned the key in the lock, she was amazed to see Watson stretched out on the back of the couch, sleeping in the sun. How had he snuck in? What if he'd gotten into another fight?

But there was Faja, curled into a furry ball by the fireplace, the picture of domestic bliss. The Ragdoll yawned delicately and padded toward her in greeting.

Faith examined her briefly and saw no injuries or sign of a fracas.

For his part, Watson opened his eyes and turned to stare out the window.

"Brooding, are we?" Faith asked, moving to the couch. She stroked his sleek black head. "I don't know how you got back inside. But don't worry. This is just a temporary arrangement." She pulled one of Watson's favorite snacks from her jacket pocket. "This is for you for being such a gentleman and not eating our guest."

When Faja twined around her ankles and looked up expectantly, Faith slipped the Ragdoll a treat too. Then she hung up her jacket and kicked off her shoes. She'd have a cup of tea and a bite to eat before returning to the library.

She smiled when Faja began pacing in front of the couch, peering up at Watson and pawing the red jingle ball that Watson liked to chase around the house.

Faith went into the kitchen and put a kettle on the stove. As she waited for the water to boil, she gazed out the window. She loved this little haven with the gardens and the green woods beyond her window. On quiet nights, she could hear the ocean lapping the shore. Now, nearly noon, birdsong drifted through the slightly raised window.

She heard another sound too—someone was coming. She pulled the white curtain aside. Wolfe's blue BMW. The cottage wasn't far from the manor, but Wolfe occasionally drove, especially if he was on his way to an appointment or in a hurry.

Her heart skipping, she fixed her hair as she hurried to the front door.

"Marlene says I just missed you." A quick smile lightened the anxious expression on his face. "Do you have a minute?"

"Of course." Her stomach was doing that flip thing that felt like hunger, but it wasn't. "I've just put the kettle on. I'm having tea, but there's coffee too."

"Tea's fine. Whatever you're having." He stepped inside, bringing in the subtle aroma of his woodsy cologne. "What's this?" he asked in surprise when Faja peered docilely up at him. "Watson has company."

"I offered to take care of Declan's pet temporarily. Marlene knows. I hope it's okay."

Wolfe angled his head as he regarded Faja. "She's a pretty thing."

"I found her in the Twain suite all caged up—and hungry," she said over her shoulder as she hurried to fix the tea. "I didn't have the heart to take her to the kennels."

Faith prepared two cups and carried them into the living room. "As nice as those kennels are, a cat like Faja shouldn't be cooped up all day, and Annie doesn't have the time to keep an eye on her."

Wolfe stroked Watson, who had climbed down from the back of the sofa to settle beside him.

Faja had hopped up onto the chair several feet away to watch.

"They seem to have gotten over their first impressions," Wolfe remarked.

Faith nodded. "I'm so relieved."

He took a swallow of the tea and was quiet for a moment, the worried expression returning to his handsome features. "We may have a situation on our hands," he said slowly.

Faith leaned forward. The moment she'd seen his expression, she knew something was up. "What do you mean?"

"Chief Garris was here today." Wolfe set the cup down on the table. "They've completed the initial autopsy."

"What did they find?"

"They're not confirming a heart attack," Wolfe answered. "Apparently, they discovered something in Declan's blood they can't identify."

"You mean something that might have killed him? Some sort of . . ." She couldn't bring herself to say the word *poison*.

"It could be anything," Wolfe said hastily. "Some condition they simply can't confirm with the limited facilities available in Lighthouse Bay. So they're sending the samples to Boston for a closer analysis."

"How long will it take to get the results?" Faith asked.

"It could be as soon as sometime today."

"What happens now?"

"We need to sit tight until we hear the results," Wolfe replied. "The police have located Declan's brother. Colin Kilpatrick will be arriving soon to identify the body. I've offered him a room at the manor until the situation is sorted out."

Faith's mind whirled with the news. "You don't think . . ."

"It's too early to think anything," he said firmly. "But I wanted you to know."

They were silent for a moment.

Faith glanced at Wolfe and noticed that he still appeared worried. "Is there something else?"

Wolfe sighed. "Declan had an envelope in his pocket addressed to B. M."

Watson's purr stopped, and birdsong ceased. Faith held her breath. When her wall clock suddenly chimed the hour, it cut the air like a blow.

"B. M. could be anyone," Wolfe said, swallowing, "but the chief is asking about Brooke."

9

The all-day poetry seminar had come to an end. Guests began streaming into the library, full of excitement and anxious to check out poetry volumes and authoritative materials about their favorite poets.

The patrons kept Faith busy—but not busy enough to keep worry at bay after Wolfe's earlier visit. What did it all mean?

Faith was jolted out of her thoughts when the Morrissey sisters approached her.

"William Cullen Bryant felt that the great spring of poetry is emotion," Madeline declared out of the blue. Her eyes sparkled behind gold-rimmed glasses. "He said, 'The most beautiful poetry is that which takes the strongest hold of the feelings.'"

Corinna rested a hand on her sister's arm as though to temper her enthusiasm.

"Bryant was an amazing man," Madeline went on, her springy curls dancing around her animated face. "He was a poet and one of the nation's leading newspaper editors, and he practiced law from 1816 until 1825. He advocated for the rights of workers and immigrants, and his influence aided in the establishment of important civic institutions."

Guests clustered around Madeline, eagerly listening as the spontaneous lecture continued.

"And Bryant was a great role model to Walt Whitman, who called him 'one of the best poets in the world!'" Madeline stated. "Whitman's ambition was to 'give something to our literature which will be our own; with neither foreign spirit, nor imagery nor form, but adapted to our case, grown out of our associations, boldly portraying the West.'"

Dr. Morrissey, Faith rehearsed mentally, recalling her surprise upon hearing that Madeline was a prestigious educator. Her arsenal of information apparently extended to exact quotes by famous poets. But what had evoked her strange comment after Declan collapsed? *I never wanted that to happen.* And what did Corinna's look of triumph mean?

"Come now," Corinna said, tugging her sister's arm. "Enough of poetry for today."

The last of the guests filed out, and stillness descended on the library.

Faith longed for peace and quiet, but Wolfe had asked her to join the guests for dinner. As she closed the library door, she remembered his ominous words: *The chief is asking about Brooke.*

On her way to dinner, she stopped in the Great Hall Gallery to briefly view the ocean through the French doors that opened onto the loggia. The sun had lowered, but the April evening still held its light, glinting orange and gold on the dark waves in a timeless benediction. She drew a sustaining breath and went on.

Suddenly there was a commotion—voices and something crashing.

Faith turned to see Laura with an empty tray in her hands. She was staring in horror at the scattered fragments of dishes that had fallen to the tiled floor and splattered on a young man in a dark-gray jacket. Laura must have bumped into him.

The man jumped back.

"Oh no!" Laura cried, eyes wide. "I'm so sorry! Are you okay?"

The man seemed as startled as Laura as he brushed the front of his slacks, which were lightly spattered with what looked like cream. "I'm fine."

Marlene rushed over to them. "Mr. Kilpatrick, are you all right?"

Kilpatrick. The man had to be Declan's younger brother, Colin. As Faith studied him, she realized he didn't resemble Declan at all. Colin was of medium height and slender build, and his thick, unruly hair of a burnished copper color curled at his neckline. Colin's hazel eyes were nothing like his brother's coal-black ones.

Marlene pressed in between the young man and the trembling housekeeper. "Laura, how many times have I told you to watch for traffic before you come bounding through the room?"

Colin knelt down and began picking up shattered pieces of china. "It was my fault. I wasn't paying attention to where I was going." His tenor voice had a breathy quality that made him seem suddenly younger than Faith had first assumed.

Faith liked that he defended Laura, who was known to be a bit on the awkward side.

To be fair, Laura's mishaps were far fewer than when she'd first started working at the manor.

"I'm really sorry," Colin said as he continued helping Laura gather the broken china, their heads bent together over the mess.

Faith stepped gingerly into the fray to collect the bowls that had not been broken.

Wolfe suddenly appeared, quickly taking in the scene. "I see we've had a little accident. Is everyone all right?"

The others nodded.

Wolfe put a hand on Colin's shoulder. "Mr. Kilpatrick is staying with us to handle his brother's affairs," he explained to the small assembled group. He turned to Colin. "We hope you'll be comfortable here."

"I don't plan to stay long enough to get comfortable," he said.

The retort took Faith by surprise.

Wolfe seemed taken off guard but only for a moment. "For as long as you are in Lighthouse Bay, you are welcome at the manor," he said smoothly. "By the way, you've already met our assistant manager, Marlene Russell. But let me introduce our librarian, Faith Newberry." He nodded to Laura. "And this is Laura Kettrick, a valuable member of our staff."

Faith warmed to his kind reference to Laura. When she glanced at Laura, she noticed a slight smile on her face.

"And now, I think we could all use a good meal," Wolfe suggested. He escorted Faith, Marlene, and Colin to the dining room while Laura carried the remnants of her tray to the kitchen.

When they entered the dining room, Marlene moved on to attend to some details, and the others took their seats at an empty table.

Eric, the enthusiastic aspiring writer, walked over and sat down across from Faith. "Well, you were right, Miss Newberry," he said. "That impression of Mark Twain was quite good after all."

Faith remembered how Eric had told her that an effective presentation would be challenging for Declan. She was glad Declan had pulled it off so admirably.

"Yes, the performance was excellent," Wolfe chimed in. "Our guests greatly enjoyed it."

Faith watched Colin, who gave no indication that he had heard the comments about his brother. She couldn't help but notice his long, graceful hands as he ate his meal.

They said nothing for a few minutes, attending to the delectable beef stroganoff and rice pilaf on their plates.

Faith wondered about the relationship between Colin and Declan and searched for some way to break the ice. "We usually don't welcome our guests by spilling cream on them," she finally told Colin. "I hope you don't hold it against us."

"Well, I was thinking of suing—at least for the price of dry-cleaning," he said with a straight face that didn't hide a faint sparkle in his eyes. "But I am genuinely sorry for the young lady. Laura, wasn't it?"

"You rescued her from the embarrassment of the moment," Faith said. "We're all very fond of Laura. She's a sweet young woman. She'll be fine."

Eric suddenly broke in. "I hear you're Mr. Ames's brother." He lowered his gaze politely. "Sorry about what happened. It's a real shame."

Colin nodded.

Eric paused, then asked, "Are you an actor too?"

Colin took a drink of his water before responding. "No. Declan's the actor in the family."

"What do you do?" Wolfe asked.

"I'm studying to be a veterinary technologist," Colin answered. "I find animals are often superior to humans. Like Whitman, 'I think I could turn and live with animals.'"

He softened Whitman's disparaging quote with a shrug, but Faith was surprised by it and wondered if it reflected his opinion of people in general or perhaps his brother. "One of my best friends in Lighthouse Bay is a veterinarian," she remarked. "She owns a clinic in town and sees to the needs of our pets here at the manor. Do you practice in Boston?"

Colin shook his head. "I've just earned my bachelor's degree in veterinary technology, and I'm working toward qualifying as a technologist."

"It takes time, I'm sure," Faith said.

"And money," Colin said. "But the hours I spent at local pounds and free clinics to earn my tuition gave me good experience."

Obviously, there was no family money if Colin had to work his way through school. Another point in his favor. Faith's heart went out to this hardworking young man who had just lost his brother, and she felt compelled to extend her condolences. "We are all stunned and saddened by your brother's death. It must be a terrible blow to you."

Colin studied his water glass, his expression inscrutable. "We were never close," he finally admitted. "The fact is, we haven't seen each other in years. I wouldn't be here now if it wasn't for . . ." His voice trailed off.

Faith felt a pang of sadness. What had happened to cause a rift between the brothers? And what regrets must Colin be feeling now that there were no more chances to seek reconciliation?

Her reverie was interrupted when Brooke and Laura appeared at their table with the dessert. Brooke held a tray of crystal dishes, and Laura began serving the caramel-cheesecake custard.

Laura smiled shyly as she placed a dish in front of Colin. "I'll try not to spill it in your lap," she said, her cheeks growing pink.

Faith smiled. Not so long ago Laura would have been completely tongue-tied in front of Colin, but now she was flirting with him. Too bad Declan's younger brother wouldn't be staying long—well, at least not any longer than he had to, apparently.

"No worries here," Colin said warmly. "It looks delicious."

"Brooke's special recipe," Laura said with a nod at the head chef.

When Colin glanced up at Brooke, Faith saw something flash in the young man's eyes. Surprise? Appreciation? Or a spark of recognition?

Brooke smiled and moved down to the next guest with Laura following.

Brooke had outdone herself again with the dessert, but Faith barely tasted it as she thought about what she'd just witnessed. Was she imagining things, or had Colin recognized Brooke? She scolded herself for getting carried away. Yet why was she feeling an overwhelming sense of dread?

When dinner was winding down and the guests began returning to their suites, Wolfe stepped out of the room to take a phone call.

A few minutes later, he returned and pulled Faith aside. "The results of the autopsy are in," he said quietly.

"What did they learn?" she asked, though she feared the answer.

Wolfe ran a hand through his dark hair peppered with gray. "They found a potentially lethal substance in Declan's body—something that can mimic a heart attack."

Faith gasped. "What was it?"

"Something called Ziophaine. It's a powerful muscle relaxer. They're trying to determine the source and how it got into his system."

Faith could feel her limbs grow cold. "Do you mean that

someone . . ." The terrible word eluded her. That someone could have deliberately poisoned the actor seemed unbelievable.

Wolfe drew in a long breath. "Declan might have taken some medication with Ziophaine in it and not known its lethal qualities. Or he may have known and overdosed himself. The police will be looking into his medical records."

"But what if someone really is responsible for his death?"

"They're doing some more testing," Wolfe answered, "and there will be an investigation."

"How terrible," Faith said.

"Marlene will break the news to Colin tonight," Wolfe said. "We hope he'll have some information that may help."

"I hope so too."

"The chief is going to talk to Brooke," Wolfe said. "I think it would help if you went along."

She searched his face. The letter found on the body, the letter addressed to B. M. Did they really think Brooke could have anything to do with what happened? "Of course I'll go with her, but what possible connection could she have to Declan?" she asked, hearing the tremor in her voice.

"Maybe none," Wolfe said, stress visible in his eyes. He gazed at her tenderly, turning only at the sound of footsteps as Chief Garris approached. He nodded to the chief and squeezed her hand. "Go with the chief. I'll call you later."

Faith was glad for the police chief's initial silence as they walked toward the kitchen, where Brooke would be cleaning up after dinner.

"Maybe you should have a look at this first," Garris said after they'd gone several paces down the hall. He stopped and handed her a small, unsealed envelope printed with the initials *B. M.*

Faith removed the paper from the envelope with trembling fingers. She unfolded the letter and studied the broad, loopy script.

"True love is the only heart disease that is best left to 'run on'—the only affection of the heart for which there is no help, and none desired."

I find I can brook no more delay in search of my healing.

"Poetic," the chief said with a raised eyebrow.

"It should be," Faith said, refolding the letter with amazement. "All but the last sentence is a direct quote from Mark Twain."

"But it's that last sentence that makes me pretty sure it was intended for Brooke Milner," Garris said. "The use of her name, I mean—though it's spelled differently."

Faith's legs felt like lead weights as they walked the remaining distance to the kitchen and went in.

Brooke was standing at the counter. She appeared small and vulnerable and young. She stared at a space beyond her. Small beads of sweat stood out on her forehead, making tendrils of her short blonde hair cling to her temples. She glanced up, taking them both in.

The chief approached and handed Brooke the envelope. "Mr. Ames had this in his possession," he told her in a quiet voice. "We think it may be meant for you."

Faith watched with a sinking heart as Brooke read the message.

Brooke set the paper down on the counter with careful precision. After a few seconds, she drew a breath and sighed. "It must be meant for me. It sounds a lot like the others."

The others? Faith shot her a look of astonishment.

"I hoped that he wouldn't . . ." Brooke shook her head. "I mean, I couldn't believe it when he showed up here."

"You knew Declan?" Faith asked softly.

Brooke nodded. "But it was such a long time ago. Ten years."

"How did you know him?" Garris asked.

"We dated for a short time when I was in Boston," Brooke explained.

"Then I ended it and asked him to leave me alone."

Faith recalled Laura's words. *At least now he won't be coming around and bothering Brooke anymore.* She had assumed Declan was bothering Brooke about his special diet. But obviously, it had been more than that.

Faith could see that Brooke's eyes were about to brim over. She knew there had been someone special long ago—someone Brooke didn't talk about. She could go on for hours about the string of boyfriends she'd dated in Lighthouse Bay and about some romantic figure that lived only in her dreams or in romantic novels. But she had never mentioned an actor named Declan Ames—or Kilpatrick.

"The results of the autopsy came back," the chief broke in. "A powerful muscle relaxer called Ziophaine was found in Mr. Ames's system. It is potentially lethal."

"I thought he had a heart attack," Brooke said, frowning.

"Ziophaine can mimic a heart attack," Garris replied. "Right now, we're attempting to verify the source and how it ended up in Mr. Ames's system."

Faith realized she was holding her breath as the import of the words reflected in Brooke's ashen face.

Brooke gasped, eyes suddenly wide. "You're not thinking that I had something to do with his death, are you?" She shot bewildered glances at Faith and Garris.

Feeling an outpouring of sympathy and affection for her friend, Faith rushed to Brooke's side. "Of course we don't think that." But even as Faith said the words, her heart sank. Brooke had prepared special meals for Declan, and Garris would realize that she could have easily tampered with his food if she had wanted to. Faith pushed away the terrible thought. The chief couldn't possibly consider Brooke a suspect.

Garris retrieved the letter from the counter and faced Brooke. "You may have knowledge that is important to this investigation. You must tell us anything you can that will assist us in figuring out what happened to Mr. Ames." He folded the letter and tucked it into his pocket. "We'll be in touch."

10

Faith arrived at the Candle House Library early the next morning.

She had phoned Eileen to fill her in on what had been happening at the manor, and they had agreed that a meeting of the book club must take place as quickly as possible. So, before the workday began for any of them, Eileen herded Faith, Brooke, and Midge to the small table in her office and closed the door behind them.

"I'm sorry," Brooke said softly. She appeared pale but composed as she wrapped her hands around the steaming mug of coffee that Eileen had ready and waiting. "I should have told you about Declan right away."

"This isn't your fault, honey," Eileen said, draping an arm around Brooke's shoulders and sitting down next to her.

"But if I had only said something," Brooke responded. "Maybe it wouldn't have happened."

Faith, seated on the other side of Brooke, shook her head. "It wouldn't have made a difference. Declan didn't have a heart attack because you turned him down. He was poisoned by something the Boston coroner's lab called Ziophaine."

"I've never heard of it," Eileen said. She picked up her ever-present knitting and set to work.

"Nor have I," Midge said, her blonde hair falling forward as she leaned across the table. "And I do have some training in pharmacology."

Atticus raised his head from Midge's lap, his Doggles bobbing comically on his small head. Midge doted on the nearsighted Chihuahua now that her two children were away at college, and she always brought him to book club meetings.

"Well, four-footed pharmacology anyway," Eileen said, laughing.

Turning to Faith, she added, "Where's that clever Watson of yours?"

"He's at home babysitting." Faith gave a wry smile.

"Babysitting?" Midge repeated.

"I was going to drop off Faja, Declan's Ragdoll cat, at the kennels, but I couldn't do it," Faith explained. "Instead, I took her to the cottage, and now Watson's keeping her company. After a little rocky start, they're getting along quite well."

"Amazing," Midge said. "So, tell us about this mystery substance that turned up in our Mark Twain impressionist."

"Apparently, Ziophaine isn't readily discernible without special testing," Faith said. "It might have been missed altogether. But somehow it got into Declan's body."

"And the chief thinks I did that?" Brooke asked incredulously. She clasped her arms over her stomach as though to hold herself together.

"No, he doesn't think that," Faith said emphatically, though Chief Garris had been pointed and stern when he had talked to Brooke and told her to make herself available for further questioning. "He needs to check out every angle and question anyone who knew the man."

"I couldn't believe it when I got Declan's first letter," Brooke said, her eyes fixed on something only she could see. "It came last week out of the blue. I don't know how he found out I was here in Lighthouse Bay. We hadn't been in touch in such a long time."

"What did you do with the letter?" Faith asked.

"I threw it out. We parted ways a decade ago, and I had no interest in him. It's true that he was special—once. He was dashing and romantic." Brooke took a deep breath. "Then I was astonished when he showed up at the manor."

"You never said anything," Faith said. "I thought you were sick or worried about Diva. I couldn't understand why you holed up in that kitchen."

"I'm sorry," Brooke said. "I just couldn't talk about it."

Eileen patted her hand. "That's all right."

"What happened when you saw Declan?" Midge asked.

"I told him right away that I wasn't interested," Brooke answered, "but he didn't want to take no for an answer. More than once he stopped by the kitchen and told me that he'd never forgotten me. He gave me notes with some nonsense about being mistaken and Eve and living in a garden."

Faith stared, entranced. It was from Twain's short story "Extracts from Adam's Diary." She recalled the quote. *After all these years, I see that I was mistaken about Eve in the beginning; it is better to live outside the Garden with her than inside it without her.*

Apparently, Declan, who had seemed to often live inside the mind of Mark Twain, was determined to have Brooke, his "Eve," back.

"Well, I pitched the notes and did my best to keep out of his way. Edna's too." Brooke frowned. "Sometimes she delivered the notes, and she gave me the most accusing looks like I was some terrible creature spoiling the man's life."

"Really?" Faith asked, surprised that Declan had asked his assistant to deliver his personal messages to Brooke. She wondered again if Edna had had romantic feelings for her boss. "Did you know Edna before? Was she Declan's publicist or assistant when you dated him?"

"No. She wasn't in the picture at all," Brooke replied. "When I knew Declan, he wasn't acting or doing impressions. He was just a guy I met at college. I don't even know what he was studying before he dropped out. He did all kinds of odd jobs, and he was always working on some scheme that was going to make him rich."

Faith had searched into Declan Kilpatrick's background but found nothing. Declan Ames, however, had a website outlining various theater groups he had participated in and his acting roles—none of which, she realized now, she had tried to authenticate. Nor had she delved into the glowing testimonials printed there. The website made no mention of the name *Kilpatrick*, as though it didn't exist at all.

"He was absolutely fixated on money," Brooke continued. "That obsession turned me off more than anything else." Her eyes misted. "I knew it had something to do with the way he was raised. He told me his parents were immigrants and never had two shillings to rub together. He claimed he wasn't going to end up that way."

The four of them were quiet for a long moment.

Eileen got up and brought the coffeepot to the table. She refilled their cups, then sat down again. "It's very sad," she said thoughtfully. "It must have been hard without a family to care about him."

Brooke nodded.

"Last night at dinner, Declan's brother seemed to recognize you," Faith said.

Brooke blinked. "His brother? That was Colin you were talking to?"

"Yes," Faith answered. "He's staying until everything's sorted out with Declan's affairs."

Brooke sighed. "I didn't recognize him. When I knew him, he was only a kid. He was always in his room reading comics." She twisted the ring on her right hand. "I felt sorry for him, especially after his parents died. How is he doing?"

"He's studying to be a veterinary technologist," Faith responded.

"Good for him," Midge said, smiling.

"What was he like?" Brooke asked.

"I thought he seemed nice," Faith said. "I especially appreciated the way he stood up for Laura when she bumped into him and spilled her tray of food all over him."

"I heard about that," Brooke said. "Laura was all moony the whole time we were serving dinner. I can't believe that was Colin."

"How did Declan get along with his brother?" Eileen asked as she continued to knit.

Brooke didn't answer right away. "Well, I didn't really see them together all that much. Like I said, Colin was only a kid. I don't think Declan made time for him. He always just shooed him off to do his homework."

"Colin said he and Declan were never close," Faith offered. "And Colin seems anxious to leave town. I don't know how he feels now that he's been told about the Ziophaine."

"How tragic," Midge said. "Even though they weren't close, it must be quite a shock for Colin."

Faith rubbed her eyes, feeling the effects of a short night. After dinner, she'd learned the startling results of the autopsy, and it was late when she had gotten back to the cottage. Finding it hard to rest, she had watched Watson and Faja play together in the living room. Eventually she'd fallen asleep on the couch after setting her alarm to make sure she wasn't late getting to the Candle House Library.

Eileen squared her shoulders and put both hands on the table. "Now, I suggest we discuss what we need to do next. If Declan didn't take the Ziophaine on purpose, he was most likely poisoned by someone who had means, motive, and opportunity. Someone at the manor. We all know Brooke is out of the question as a suspect. So, where does that leave us?"

Trust Eileen to simplify a situation and develop an action plan.

"We need to check the backgrounds of our suspects, including family members," Eileen continued. She narrowed her eyes. "What about Professor Clement George? Didn't you say there was some animosity between him and Declan?"

"Well, that first night—just before we were getting started in the library—Clement and Declan had some words," Faith answered.

"What was it about?" Midge asked.

"Something to do with Bret Harte," Faith said. "On the surface, it didn't sound all that awful, except Declan insulted the professor. He said something about his studies being a waste of time."

"We had some phone conversations when Clement was researching another project," Eileen said. "I always thought he was a proper gentleman, but first impressions can be deceiving." She made some notes on a pad. "I'll investigate your resident cowboy. I have been wondering what happened to him after he left Heatherstone."

"I'll ask my cousin to work some of her genealogical magic too," Midge said. "She loves a challenge, and she can come up with surprising results."

"I'll be interested to hear what she finds," Faith said.

"Edna is the one who was closest to Declan." Midge frowned. "She also bears some scrutiny, I should say." She fondled her dog's ears. "Right, Atticus?"

The little dog yipped as if in response.

"We can't rule her out as a suspect." Faith drew a contemplative breath. "But there's something going on with the Morrissey sisters that puzzles me too."

The fact was, there could be any number of suspects—some that came quickly to mind, but what about the other guests? Someone completely unknown and unsuspected could have a reason to want Declan dead. It was chilling. But so was the idea that the actor might have killed himself.

"Well," Eileen said, glancing at her watch, "our time is up. We all have work to do. Let's keep our eyes and ears open."

The Candle House Book Club had been through a lot together. They had sleuthed out clues and found answers to perplexing crimes before. This one, though, had Brooke squarely in the middle of it. It was all the more reason to stick together and solve the mystery as soon as possible.

Faith said goodbye to Midge and Atticus and thanked Eileen. Then she gave Brooke a reassuring hug. "Try not to worry. It's going to be all right."

"I'll try," Brooke said, "but everyone's going to be gossiping about me and giving me suspicious looks."

"No they won't," Faith told her. "But if they do, we'll sic Watson—and Atticus—on them."

Unfortunately, there will be gossip, Faith thought as she drove away from the Candle House Library. It was unavoidable.

She rolled the window down. The air was still chilly, and despite the greening beauty of the countryside, it was hard to feel the abandon and lure of spring.

The cat finished his morning wash and leaped up onto his favorite perch on the back of the couch. The sun came in the window just right, and he could feel it warming his back.

Near the fireplace, the feline interloper delicately swiped her paws across her funny face.

His human had left him right after breakfast and before he could dash out through the open door. He'd planned to sneak out and have a prowl through the garden this morning, but he could take a nap instead. Or he could talk to the fluffy-tailed animal flounced on the rug by the fireplace. But she didn't have a whole lot to say. Just some anemic mewling now and then.

The interloper couldn't help that she was an inferior species. She wasn't bad at playing games, though, he supposed. However, yesterday she had batted his favorite toy into that slot in the floor where warm air rushed through. So far, he hadn't been able to fish it out.

She stopped cleaning her fur and stared at him with that goofy look she had. She pirouetted once or twice and pounced toward him as though inviting him to play.

He ignored her and turned to gaze out the window. Surely there would be a squirrel or a bird. Sometimes the feathered ninnies would fly right up to the windowsill and sit there until he swiped at the glass with his paw. But now there was nothing.

Wait a minute. There was something. A human at the far edge of the woods—and another one who looked like a walking tree with two skinny branches.

The cat sat up erect, his whiskers twitching. Maybe they would come this way. He crouched, waiting. He knew the lady human. She was the one with her nose in the air who pulled his new housemate with a long rope. He'd never seen the man who looked like a tree. Their mouths moved, and their arms flailed like the female cat's tail.

And then the skinny human disappeared into the woods quicker than a squirrel.

Ah, well. Time for a nap.

Faith drove directly to the manor, her mind full of what she had learned about Brooke's past relationship with Declan and what it might mean in the coming days. She would prefer the serenity of her cottage rather than face the difficulty of carrying on a retreat with a criminal investigation in process, but she needed to get to work.

At least she hoped serenity reigned in her cottage. When she had left the house, the two cats had been contentedly lapping up their breakfasts, Watson stopping every few minutes to inspect Faja's progress. Or more likely, to make sure the Ragdoll wasn't about to wander over to his bowl. She'd check on them later, but the guests would expect the library to be open.

Just my luck, Faith muttered under breath. Marlene was pacing outside the library door. "Sorry I'm running a bit late," she said as she approached.

But Marlene's face didn't hold the censure Faith was expecting. Instead, the assistant manager appeared pale and nervous. She motioned impatiently for Faith to move inside, glancing around as though to ensure their privacy. "I need to talk to you." She was holding her fancy watch with the rhinestones around its face and rubbing a red indentation on her wrist.

Marlene moved toward the fireplace, jerking her head to indicate that Faith was to follow her deeper into the library. She whirled around as Faith caught up to her and set the watch on the mantel as though the timepiece had offended her.

"Is anything wrong?" Faith asked. *Silly question*, she thought. A guest had died—maybe been poisoned by someone right here in the manor. Everything was wrong.

"Yesterday when you fetched the cat from the Mark Twain Suite, did you move anything?" Marlene said. "I mean, did you happen to disturb anything—maybe in trying to capture the animal?" Her pale-green eyes were less accusing than curious.

Faith shook her head. "Faja was in her cage, and she came right out when I opened the door. I didn't have to convince her to come with me." She felt a niggling sense of dread. "She flopped in my arms, and I carried her out."

"Did you notice anything out of order? Open suitcases or drawers or anything?" Marlene touched her fingertips to her wrist again, and Faith noticed that a faint rash had developed there.

Faith searched Marlene's face for some reason for these questions. "No. I looked around a bit, but I didn't see anything wrong."

"You didn't touch anything?" Marlene persisted.

"No," Faith repeated, irritated. "Well, I did check for some kibble or other food for Faja. She was hungry, and it didn't seem like she'd been fed for several hours."

"Housekeeping was ordered not to go in there until further notice," she said, talking more to herself than to Faith. "You were the only one in there."

The Mark Twain Suite had been picture-perfect when Faith had glanced around at the amazing furnishings. It had appeared as though no one had been staying in the room. "I didn't disturb anything. What is this all about?"

Marlene pressed her lips together. She paced a few strides forward and returned. "It couldn't be the housekeeping staff," she muttered. "They were ordered not to enter the suite until after the police inspected it. Besides, they wouldn't have left it in that condition."

"What is it?" Faith asked impatiently.

"I just took Chief Garris and Officer Laddy up there," Marlene answered. "Unless Mr. Ames was a real slob, someone has been in that suite going through his things."

Faith stared in stunned surprise.

Seconds ticked by as the import of the news sank in.

"You mean someone broke into the suite?" Faith finally asked.

"No," Marlene said. She pursed her lips, and now an accusatory glint sparked in her eyes. "The suite was unlocked. In your haste, you must have left it open."

Faith couldn't believe what she was hearing. She started to protest but stopped to search her memory again. She had clutched Faja under her arm, along with the leash, so she'd have a free hand to lock the suite, and she had locked it. She was sure of it. "I did not leave it open. I know I locked it, and I returned the key to you before going home with Faja."

Marlene swallowed a quick retort. "Then how—?" Her brow furrowed in thought. "How did someone just walk into the suite and ransack it?"

"I don't know," Faith replied. Was it possible that someone had come in behind her? Had they snuck in and simply waited for her to leave the suite with Faja before searching through Declan's belongings? She'd seen no one, and she'd heard nothing.

Marlene released a frustrated breath. "Well, however it happened, the fact is, someone was in there looking for something, and we've got to get to the bottom of this mess one way or the other." She turned around sharply and left the library.

11

Faith stared at Marlene's retreating back, her mind whirling with the latest news. What could someone want inside the suite that Declan Ames had occupied? And what did it have to do with the actor's death? Was there no limit to the number of mysteries occurring all around her?

There would be no time to worry and wonder about it now because guests were entering the library.

She greeted the Amboys, who strode in almost on the heels of Marlene, their bright faces in contrast to Faith's dark thoughts.

"We decided to spend some time in the gorgeous library this morning before heading into your charming town," Constance said.

"If I can be of any assistance, please don't hesitate to ask," Faith said warmly.

"I'm searching for a few reference books," William said. "I was wondering if you might point me in the right direction."

"Of course." Faith escorted William to the reference section.

After locating the books for him, Faith walked to her desk. With all that had been happening, she was getting behind on her correspondence and filing.

She had just sat down when Eric suddenly appeared at her desk—seemingly out of nowhere. "Hello, Miss Newberry," he said, drawing close with a charming smile. He moved with quick ease—like a dancer or a skater.

His jovial manner was jarring after the exchange with Marlene that had left Faith with a gnawing in the pit of her stomach. But she mustn't let her worry affect her interactions with the guests. "Good morning. Is there something I can help you with?"

"I'm looking for a book by William Dean Howells." Eric stroked his mustache with his thumb and index finger. "*The Rise of Silas Lapham.* It's a realist novel that highlights Howell's rejection of sentimental romantic novels."

Faith got up and ushered him over to the fiction section. "Here it is," she said, removing it from the bookcase and handing it to him.

"Thank you." As Eric accepted the volume, he took a step closer, his aftershave wafting toward her. "I hear that Declan Ames may not have suffered a heart attack after all," he said in a secretive whisper. "Is it true someone poisoned him?"

Faith swallowed hard. It was inevitable that the guests would be talking about Declan, but she had hoped it wouldn't begin so soon. "That has not been determined," she said firmly. "The investigation is ongoing, Mr. McCandless."

"Please call me Eric." He smiled. "When I hear Mr. McCandless, I think you're speaking to my father."

Avoiding the use of his name, she responded as politely as she could. "I don't think it helps matters to speculate. How Mr. Ames died is a matter for the authorities. They are handling it, and there's no reason to become sidetracked. We want everyone to enjoy their time at the manor."

"Absolutely. And an impressive place it is." Eric made a small bow. "You have been most helpful, Miss Newberry." He paused. "It's Faith, isn't it?"

Faith found his flirtatious behavior a bit disconcerting. But he had asked her to call him by his first name. She nodded without confirming her given name. "Is there anything else I can help you with?"

He smiled and held up the book. "Thank you. As I said, you have been most helpful." He spun around on his heel and was gone.

The morning passed quickly with a sporadic flow of guests coming and going.

Shortly after lunch, Clement strode through the library doors, ducking his head as most tall men do, whether necessary or not. He was dressed casually in jeans and an open-collared blue shirt. His barrel chest strained the buttons of a brown suede jacket as he browsed a long section of shelves, occasionally nodding to a passing guest.

Eventually, Clement approached the glass cases containing the first editions of *Tom Sawyer Abroad* and *Adventures of Huckleberry Finn*.

Faith wished she was close enough to read his expression, but a side view revealed only broad sloping shoulders and bushy sideburns. She wondered what he was thinking as he lingered at the accompanying display highlighting Mark Twain's accomplishments.

What was the contention between Clement and Declan? Maybe she had misinterpreted that exchange between them three nights ago when Declan had derided Clement's work on the Harte biography. Why had Declan nosed into the conversation and told Clement to consider another project? What had he meant by that scornful remark about Clement writing something he could own?

The display Faith had put together did not address the bitter rift between Mark Twain and Bret Harte, but she had researched it. The two authors had become friends after they first met in San Francisco in 1864. They had a brief falling-out after that, but their bitter rivalry was permanently sealed when they collaborated on the disastrous play *Ah Sin*.

The reason for the rift between Twain and Harte remained a matter of speculation. Possible causes included professional jealousy, disagreements over the revisions of the play, and a request Harte made for a loan, which Twain refused. Whatever the reason, the two writers never spoke to each other after 1877.

In 1878, Twain wrote a letter to William Dean Howells, fuming that Harte was "a liar, a thief, a swindler, a snob, a sot, a sponge, a coward . . . How do I know? By the best of all evidence, personal experience."

Faith pulled up the article she had found earlier and reread it on the computer screen. Twain said, "Bret Harte is the most contemptible, poor little soulless blatherskite that exists on the planet today." It was precisely the epithet Declan had quoted three nights ago.

So, had Declan's barb merely given voice to Twain's opinion of Harte? Or was there some personal animosity between Declan and Clement?

When she glanced up from the screen, Clement was gone. In fact, everyone was gone except for Madeline, who stood by the fireplace alone, resting a hand on the carved mantel. Her perennially present sister, Corinna, was nowhere to be seen.

Madeline seemed to be studying the painting just above the fireplace—an original oil in swirling tones. Faith watched as the woman glanced around from time to time and returned her gaze to the painting. But suddenly, she took her hand down from the mantel and opened her tapestry bag. Something flashed, its beam reaching across the room, and Madeline hurried out of the library.

A moment later, something pinged in the back of Faith's mind. What was that flash when Madeline opened her tapestry bag? Faith recalled her conversation with Marlene by the fireplace. The assistant manager had set her watch on the mantel as she interrogated Faith about the key to the Mark Twain Suite. Had Marlene forgotten to take it when she left?

Faith thought back, but she couldn't remember Marlene picking up the watch. The assistant manager had just gone on scratching her wrist and shaking her head over the unlocked door to the Twain suite. That's what that flashing was about—the circle of rhinestones around the face of the watch. It was highly doubtful that the stones were diamonds. Marlene was a careful dresser but not one to parade high-end fashions or valuable jewelry.

Could it be? Had the prestigious lady of letters known for her
erudite lectures taken the watch? Perhaps she intended to take it to
the lost and found. Faith chewed the inside of her cheek. But wouldn't
it be more logical to bring it to the librarian right here in the room?
Unless, seeing Faith intent on her computer screen, Madeline hadn't
wanted to bother her.

She pondered the strange episode, wondering what to do. Should
she go after Madeline and let her know she'd been spotted? Report
the possible theft to Marlene? Wait and see what Madeline's intention
was? Perhaps she knew it belonged to Marlene and had already gone
to return it to her. Or she might be taking it at this moment to the
front desk.

As Faith debated, she went to the fireplace to confirm what she
thought she had seen. Indeed, the watch was gone. As she stood staring
at the empty spot on the mantel, her cell phone vibrated in her pocket.
Eileen's name came up on the monitor.

"Are you busy?" her aunt asked.

From the note of intrigue in Eileen's voice, Faith knew something
was going on. "A minute ago, there were several guests demanding my
attention, but now the place is quiet as a church."

"Well, I've been looking into our Professor George. I couldn't
get much out of the people at Heatherstone College, except that he's
no longer working there." Eileen paused. "But I did get ahold of a
friend of mine—a former colleague. She taught at the college before
her retirement."

"What did she tell you?" Faith asked.

"Nothing yet," Eileen admitted. "She wants to catch up, so I
thought I'd run over and see her later. She lives in Bullard. Could you
get away around four?"

Faith considered. Most of the guests would likely be out on a day
like today. Brilliant sunshine, balmier than usual for April. Midge had
mentioned that Samuel Peak, the manor's head groom, was taking a

group of horseback riders out on the trails following Clement's short talk on Bret Harte's Western novels. The discussion was to be held in the music room at three, which was an hour or so away.

"I think that will work," Faith said. "And I'd love to go with you. Do you think your friend will have any information on our Harte enthusiast?"

"What Diane Lindquist doesn't know about Heatherstone probably isn't worth knowing," Eileen said cryptically. "I'll pick you up at your cottage at four."

"Good. That will give me time to change clothes and feed Watson and Faja."

"Are those two still getting along?" Eileen asked.

"So far, so good. See you soon."

Faith disconnected, then delved into a questionnaire for the chamber of commerce. Before she could finish the form, a few guests entered and started browsing the library. She attended to their needs, but her mind kept returning to Madeline and the watch.

When a text came in from the assistant manager saying she thought she'd left her watch in the library by mistake and asking Faith to hold it for her, it was clear that Madeline hadn't contacted Marlene.

She called the front desk. Cara, the young clerk, reported that no one had turned in a watch of any description.

Faith felt a sinking in her stomach. She must talk to Madeline and give her a chance to explain. She stepped out and headed for the grand staircase that led to the guest rooms.

Laura appeared at the base of the stairs, carefully balancing a tray. The slim young woman turned at the sound of Faith's footsteps. "Hi," she said and returned her focus to the laden tray containing an individual silver teapot, a floral china cup, and a plate containing cherry tarts.

"That looks lovely," Faith said. "Room service?"

"I guess so," Laura replied. "Marlene asked me to deliver a tray to Miss Grimmell before I left. I have the rest of the day off." She smiled.

"Why did she ask you to do that?"

"Marlene's worried about her," Laura answered.

"Did something happen?"

"Miss Grimmell missed lunch and breakfast, and she seems to be hiding away in her room. Or maybe she's been driving into town to eat. Anyway, it must be really awful for her to lose her boss like that."

"It's very thoughtful of our assistant manager," Faith said, meaning it. With Declan's death, Edna had to feel at loose ends. After all, she'd lost her job—if not a friend. "I was on my way up to see another guest, so I'll go with you." She gave Laura a reassuring smile. "Are you all right with that tray?"

"It's not heavy," she said with a grin. "And I'll watch out for handsome strangers."

"He is handsome, isn't he?" Faith teased, remembering how Laura and Colin had met. "With his unruly hair and mysterious eyes."

Laura blushed. "He said I was lucky to work in a nice place like this," she said softly. "I told him I knew I was."

"I think he likes you," Faith said. "He sure was gallant the way he stood up for you when Marlene snapped at you."

Laura blushed a deeper pink. She was quiet a long moment as they climbed the stairs. "It must be hard to lose a brother."

Faith sighed. "Yes. Even if you didn't like him much and haven't been on speaking terms." *Maybe especially then*, she thought. She wanted a chance to talk to Colin about Declan—which she was sure the police would do. They'd also want to know why someone had been searching through Declan's belongings in his room.

"Here's Miss Grimmell's suite," Laura said.

"Your hands are full, so I'll knock." Faith rapped firmly.

It had to be a full thirty seconds before the door opened. Edna wore a black-and-white checked jacket over black pants. She was in her stocking feet, her shoes tossed off just inside the door. A purse and car keys lay haphazardly on a table in the foyer as though she had recently returned from an outing. She peered suspiciously at her visitors. Her eyes were bloodshot.

"I didn't order anything," Edna said crossly before Laura could explain.

Faith noticed Laura's hands trembling on the tray, so she spoke up for her. "Ms. Russell asked Laura to bring you something," she said gently. "You haven't been coming to meals. She wanted to make sure you're all right."

"Are you trying to poison me too?" Edna hissed.

Faith was so stunned by the words that she couldn't speak. She stared into Edna's accusing eyes underlined by shadow. The woman seemed to have discounted any possibility that Declan had brought about his own death and believed he had been deliberately poisoned.

"It's that chef," Edna went on. "She put something in his food, and now she wants to kill me too. I told him coming here was a mistake."

Her voice rose with each syllable, and Faith worried that guests still in their rooms could hear. A man had rounded the corner and was coming toward them.

"I warned him not to go near her, but she had him going crazy." Edna's normally controlled voice shook, and her eyes flashed. "I saw them hiding away in the kitchen. The police should have arrested her by now."

"Miss Grimmell," Faith said, trying to penetrate the irrational ravings. Did the woman really believe what she was saying? She was a suspect herself and had been interrogated by the police. Were these the expressions of grief—the need to blame someone for irreparable loss? Faith wondered what the drama was about. Perhaps Edna had been in love with her boss after all.

Edna suddenly flung out an arm and shoved the tray, sending it flying at the man who had just reached the door.

Without another word, Edna slammed her door shut, sending waves of reverberating sound through the air.

Colin stood there, shoes spattered with tea.

"What on earth is going on?" Marlene raced down the hall. She stopped and gaped at the mess—broken china, smashed cherry tarts, and tea spilling from the upended silver pot.

Faith couldn't believe it. How was it possible that this was happening again? Another spilled tray, a shocked and trembling Laura, and Colin, the unsuspecting passerby?

"Edna knocked the tray out of Laura's hands," Faith told Marlene, not wanting the young housekeeper to be blamed for clumsiness. "Unfortunately, Colin was walking by at the time."

Colin nodded, then bent to scoop up the contents of the tray, which surprisingly took only a moment. The man had amazing dexterity. "I'll take this back to the kitchen for you," he offered as he glanced at Laura.

"Okay, I'll take care of this," Marlene said, putting a hand on Laura's shivering shoulder. "You go on back to work."

As Colin and Laura walked away, Faith heard Colin ask Laura if she was going horseback riding with the group later.

Marlene turned to Faith with a frustrated exhalation. "I'm late for a meeting. I'll have to deal with Miss Grimmell later."

Before Faith could tell Marlene about her watch, the assistant manager zipped down the hallway.

Faith sighed. Addressing the matter of the watch would have to wait. Marlene had more pressing concerns at the moment.

And Faith had an appointment with Eileen to investigate Clement. She hoped Eileen's friend would be able to shed some light on the professor and his rivalry with Declan. How long had the two men been foes?

Faith shivered as she wondered once more if Clement was capable of murder.

12

Faith had just finished pouring food into separate bowls for Watson and Faja when Eileen arrived at the cottage.

"I'll be home soon," Faith told them. "Be good, you two."

Both cats stopped eating and gave her innocent looks.

Faith laughed. She grabbed her fleece jacket, knowing that it would get chilly at sundown, locked the cottage, and hurried to her aunt's car.

Eileen rolled down the window and smiled. "Hop in."

Faith jumped into the passenger side and leaned back against the seat. "What a day. It's been a regular roller coaster." She turned to her aunt. "But I'm glad to see your smiling face."

Eileen reached over to pat Faith's arm and zoomed off.

Her aunt was no daredevil, but she was anything but sedate behind the wheel. When Eileen had traded in her beige Camry and bought a ruby-red Ford Mustang, she surprised everyone. Faith knew Eileen had an adventurous streak and loved her for it. Most of the time, anyway.

"So, who hasn't been smiling today?" Eileen asked as they headed for the small community of Bullard.

"Marlene for one. She was waiting for me when I came back from our meeting at Candle House this morning, and she wasn't exactly happy."

"What is it this time?" Eileen said.

"It seems someone got into Declan's suite before the police to search for something," Faith replied. "Marlene wanted to know what I saw when I went inside to pick up Faja."

"Which was?"

"Nothing. I mean, nothing out of order. No spilled suitcases or drawers left open. I was impressed that Declan was such a tidy housekeeper. Unless cleaning up after him was also on Edna's to-do list."

Eileen frowned. "Very odd. Someone must have come in after you and gone through his things. I wonder what he—or she—was after."

"Yes," Faith agreed with a sigh. "A lot of strange things have been happening. It's hardly been a retreat. More like a major skirmish."

"Oh no. What else is going on?"

"Edna accused Brooke of trying to poison her." Faith briefly related what had happened when she and Laura went to deliver the tray to Edna's suite.

Eileen shook her head. "Poor Brooke."

"Edna said something strange while she was ranting and raving and knocking the tray from Laura's hands. She said, 'I told him coming here was a mistake.' She obviously meant Declan. Then she said she'd warned him not to go near Brooke and that she'd seen him and Brooke 'hiding away in the kitchen.'"

"But that's ridiculous," Eileen protested. "Brooke didn't want anything to do with him. Do you think Declan confided in Edna about wanting to see Brooke, even before they arrived at the manor?"

"She definitely knows much more than she's saying."

"Someone sure does," Eileen said.

"Clement came into the library this afternoon," Faith remarked after they had driven in silence for several minutes.

"Did he talk to you?" Eileen asked.

"No. He spent quite a long time examining the Mark Twain display. He might have wanted to see if anything related to Bret Harte, but I didn't include anything about the feud between the two authors."

"How did Clement react to the display?"

"I wish I could have read his expression, but his face was averted," Faith said. "And those bushy sideburns didn't help either."

"Clement seems to have a pretty good grip on himself," Eileen said. "He keeps his own counsel, and his face doesn't betray much."

"Still waters run deep," Faith murmured.

"Did Clement give his lecture on Harte yet?"

"Yes, he made his presentation a little while ago," Faith answered. "Now Samuel is taking the group horseback riding. I heard Colin ask Laura if she was going on the ride when they left Marlene and me at Edna's door."

Eileen glanced at her. "Really? Do you think they're sweet on each other?"

"I believe so. For Laura's sake, I just hope that Colin can be trusted."

The GPS indicated a turn onto the next ramp.

Eileen signaled and obeyed. "I'm looking forward to seeing Diane. It's been a long time."

"What is she like?"

"She can be a bit overbearing," Eileen admitted, "and she can level a student with a single glance. But she was a first-rate linguistics teacher. 'Lindquist the Linguist,' they used to call her."

Faith laughed.

A moment later, Eileen pulled up to a small brick home with old-fashioned shutters. Low yew bushes fronted the house, and a narrow strip of cobbles led to a red door.

It opened before Eileen could ring the bell. A tall woman wearing a striped green smock, sandals, and a long denim skirt appeared. Her white hair was piled carelessly on her head, and stray tendrils wisped about her face. A pencil was perched over her left ear, as though she'd just come from grading papers.

"Eileen, you darling!" Diane crowed, beaming. She flung her arms around Eileen. "We meet again at last." She took a step back. "And who is this you've brought with you?" Her blue eyes blazed.

Eileen smiled. "Faith Newberry, my niece and a fellow librarian. She works at Castleton Manor."

Faith extended her hand. "Ms. Lindquist, it's a pleasure. My aunt has told me so much about you," she said, feeling somewhat daunted by the larger-than-life persona.

Diane shook Faith's hand. "I'll bet she has. Believe it. It's all true.

But call me Diane. I'm old as the hills, but I like being called by my first name." She winked. "It helps me retain a shred of my girlhood."

Eileen laughed.

"Now come on in, you two." Diane ushered them inside. "I'm tickled to see you. Ah, 'tickled' is such a quaint expression. It's Middle English, fourteenth century, from *tikelen*." She shook her head. "Never mind. I can't help myself."

They followed her into a cozy sitting room with a red lounge chair and a pair of sofas with denim slipcovers. A low table designed to look like an artist's pallet had been set with two ceramic flowered cups and a matching teapot, blue napkins, and a large plate of assorted cookies.

"Let me fetch another cup. Just a minute." Diane hurried into the kitchen.

Faith and Eileen took places on one of the couches while they waited.

When Diane returned, she set the mug on the table, then gestured at the cookies. "You'll be glad to know I didn't bake them. They're store-bought but very tasty."

"Don't sell yourself short," Eileen said. "I seem to recall that you used to make a delicious pineapple upside-down cake."

"Oh, that was years ago, and I no longer bake." Diane flounced into the lounge chair and promptly put her feet up. "You pour, Eileen. I'm a complete klutz at tea parties. Klutz. Hmm. From Middle High German *kloz*. It means 'lumpy mass.'"

"I'm glad to see you haven't changed. I've missed you," Eileen said warmly. She poured cups for Diane and Faith and one for herself. "I was surprised to learn that you had settled here so near to Lighthouse Bay. I couldn't wait to see you."

"Uncle Reginald willed this cottage to me, God rest his soul," Diane said. "He was an old lobsterman, and he sold his fleet of boats and lived here until he passed away. When I learned that I'd inherited the house, you could have knocked me over with a feather." She sipped her tea.

"It's no palace, but it suits me. There's plenty of room, and it's close to the ocean—and not that far from old Heatherstone's hallowed walls."

"I'm very glad you're here," Eileen said.

"Me too," Diane said. "Have a cookie, and pass me one of those coconut puffs over there." She held out her plate.

Eileen gave her a coconut puff. "I've been around Lighthouse Bay almost all my life. I was thrilled when my niece accepted the position of librarian at Castleton Manor."

"Now there's a real palace," Diane said, leaning forward and dropping a few shreds of coconut on her lap. "One of these days I'm going to get up there for a tour. The mansion is magnificent, and the grounds with all those beautiful topiaries and gardens are a dream. Who owns it?"

"It's still in the Jaxon family. Wolfe Jaxon is a co-owner," Eileen said with a glance at Faith. "And he's doing a fine job. In addition to managing other businesses, he opens the manor for booklovers' events. There's a retreat in session now."

"Yes," Diane said. "You said something about needing my help. What can I do for you?"

"It's been kept pretty quiet for the moment, but two days ago, one of the guests at the retreat died," Eileen said. "An actor who does impressions of Mark Twain. He collapsed during his presentation."

"That's terrible," Diane remarked.

Faith explained the cause was first thought to be a heart attack but that there was evidence of a possible homicide. "The retreat is continuing as planned, but an investigation is going on to determine exactly what happened and who caused it."

Diane's face registered shock, but she quickly regained her composure. "How can I help?"

"One of the retreat guests is a man who taught at Heatherstone College some years ago," Eileen replied. "I tried to get some background on him through the college, but they weren't forthcoming with information. The only thing they confirmed was that he doesn't work there anymore."

"Who are we talking about?" Diane asked.

"Clement George," Eileen said.

Diane raised her white eyebrows and leaned forward in her chair. "George," she repeated, nodding. "I remember the name. 'Clement' isn't a common name. Or 'George' as a surname for that matter. Tall, sandy hair, and sideburns. Loves horses."

"Yes, that's him," Faith said.

"Talking about the college reminds me of the halcyon days of my departed youth." Diane sighed dramatically. "But retirement is great. Now I have the opportunity to do what a busy educator never had time for."

"So what happened?" Eileen asked, getting the conversation back on track.

"About ten years ago, Clement was dismissed from his teaching duties on the charge of plagiarism," Diane replied.

"How did it come to light?" Faith asked.

"As I recall, a student made the charge," Diane continued. "The board was divided on the matter, but Clement's contract was not renewed for the following year. To make matters even worse, his marriage fell apart during the scandal. She was a lovely young woman—a real bright light at faculty parties."

"How sad," Eileen commented.

"What happened to the student who made the charge?" Faith asked.

"He left Heatherstone too," Diane responded. "A cocky young man with messy black hair and an Irish name."

Faith drew in her breath. "Declan Kilpatrick?" It was almost a whisper.

"Why, yes," Diane said, tilting her head. "How could I have forgotten a name like that?" She shut her eyes as though to recall linguistic knowledge buried in her memory. "It's a traditional name of a saint who founded a monastery in Ireland. Supposedly, St. Declan's

Stone has been the site of many miracles." She opened her eyes and glanced from Eileen to Faith. "What is it?"

Eileen gripped her hands together in her lap. "Declan Kilpatrick is the man who died during his presentation at Castleton."

The silence that followed was almost palpable.

"You mean the two of them—Clement George and Declan Kilpatrick—were at your retreat?" Diane said, her blue eyes wide. She released the lever on her lounge chair and dropped her sandaled feet to the floor. "Astonishing."

"Yes, they were both at the manor," Faith answered. "And they belong to the same historical society. Clement teaches at a small private college near Hartford now. Declan was an actor, not an academic, but he probably participated in the society to gather background on Mark Twain."

"Do you think Clement killed Declan?" Diane said. "But ten years? Surely after all this time, Clement wouldn't murder Declan."

"You wouldn't think so," Eileen said. "But it certainly makes Clement a strong suspect."

"How exactly did he die?" Diane asked.

Eileen explained what they knew of the substance, which in large quantities was lethal. "Ziophaine is a powerful muscle relaxer prescribed for severe pain. It's very hard to detect in the body, and it can mimic the symptoms of a heart attack."

Faith shook her head. "Brooke, the head chef at the manor and a very good friend of ours, is a suspect because she prepared special meals for his restrictive diet."

"Do they have any evidence?" Diane asked. "The smoking gun, if you will."

"No," Faith said. "We've got to find out who did it because Brooke is a suspect. She was a onetime love interest of Declan's, and he was trying to woo her back. He even had a letter addressed to her in his pocket the night he died. But she would never murder him."

"The whole thing is bizarre," Eileen said. "It's even possible that Declan Ames—that's how he's billed as an impressionist—could have taken the lethal dose himself. But there was no suicide note, and he did seem to get under the skin of a lot of folks."

"I wish I could be more help," Diane said, cupping her hands around her cup. "But I can thank this Declan Kilpatrick—or Ames—for one thing."

"What is that?" Eileen asked.

"He brought you to my humble door. And I hope this is only the beginning of our reacquaintance." Diane reached over and grabbed Faith's hand. "And seeing you again, my dear, would double the pleasure."

After promising to keep in touch and get together again soon, Faith and Eileen left Diane's cottage.

They were quiet for most of the ride back to the manor in the gathering dusk.

Faith reflected on what they had learned. Was it possible that Clement had put the drug into Declan's last meal or coffee? It seemed likely that Clement blamed his nemesis for both his dismissal from Heatherstone and the ending of his marriage. But why would he wait nearly ten years to seek reprisal?

If Clement was indeed responsible, then how had he accessed a drug like Ziophaine? Even if he obtained the drug, he would have needed a small, cautious window of time in which to doctor the food Brooke had prepared and Marlene had carried to Declan's room. It seemed like a long shot.

Lights winked on all over the grounds as they drove to Faith's cottage.

When Eileen pulled into the driveway, she motioned to Wolfe walking up the cobbled path. "Looks like someone else is heading your way."

Wolfe approached the car and opened the passenger door. "Good evening, ladies."

Eileen greeted him, then turned to Faith. "I'll do some more investigating and call you tomorrow."

Faith nodded.

Wolfe helped Faith out of the car. They waved at Eileen as she drove away.

"This is a nice welcome home," Faith said. After Diane's revelations and her own chilling thoughts, his warm touch brought tremendous comfort. "I've been visiting an old friend of Eileen's in Bullard, and I have some news."

"I have some too," Wolfe said. "Let's go inside and talk if you're not too tired."

She noticed the concern in Wolfe's voice and the deepening lines in his forehead. "I'm glad you're here," she said simply.

When Faith unlocked the door, both cats were waiting in the foyer.

Watson looked at her as if to say, "It's about time you got home."

Faja sat on the mat like a doorstop, her bushy tail curled around her feet.

Wolfe gave Watson's head a pat and glanced down at Faja. "The cats seem to be getting along." He unzipped his jacket but didn't remove it.

Faja twined around his ankles and purred.

"Can I get you a cup of coffee?" Sensing his urgency, Faith added, "It will only take a minute."

"Yes, please," Wolfe said.

Faith ushered him into the living room, and he sat down on the sofa, immediately surrendering his lap to the trusting, docile Ragdoll. Then Faith hurried into the kitchen.

When Faith returned with the coffee, Wolfe gently urged Faja off his lap. "So, what did you find out from Eileen's friend?"

She handed him a mug and sat down on the couch next to him. "Thank you."

"Diane Lindquist said that Clement and Declan were both at

Heatherstone College at the same time." Faith took a sip of coffee. "About ten years ago, Declan got Clement dismissed from Heatherstone on a plagiarism charge."

As she filled him in, Faith recalled what Declan had said that first night when confronting Clement: *Maybe you should consider another project, Professor. Something you can rightfully claim as yours, that is.* Had it been Declan's way of reminding Clement that he knew the ugly secret he'd carried for over ten years? That he could ruin him among academic circles by circulating it?

Wolfe searched her face. "That certainly gives Clement a motive to murder Declan. Still, why would he wait a decade to take revenge? And why here? He and Declan belonged to the same historical society and had access to each other."

"I don't know, but there's more to a possible motive," Faith said.

"What else did you learn?" Wolfe took a drink of his coffee, then set the mug on the table.

"Diane was on staff at the college when all this broke. She also told us that Clement's marriage dissolved during the scandal." Faith shook her head. "Clement most likely blames Declan for the loss of his wife as well as his job at Heatherstone."

"I agree it's a strong motive, but did Clement have the means and the opportunity?" Wolfe asked. "After all, Ziophaine isn't found in everyone's medicine cabinet. How would Clement obtain that powerful muscle relaxer? And it wasn't something Declan would take unless he wanted to kill himself."

"If we can figure out where the drug came from or who it was prescribed for—if it was prescribed—that would certainly help."

They were quiet a long moment, their coffee cooling on the table before them.

"I wanted to let you know something else," Wolfe finally said. He pushed a hand through his hair with a weary sigh. "This situation is getting more confusing by the minute."

Faith studied his face, wishing she could make all of this go away for him. For all of them. "What is it?"

"When the police searched Declan's apartment in Hartford, they found that someone had broken in and destroyed the place," Wolfe answered. "There were pictures ripped from the walls, chairs and mattresses torn open, cupboards and drawers emptied, and clothing scattered everywhere."

Faith imagined the chaotic scene, but it didn't make sense. Someone had rummaged through Declan's belongings in the Mark Twain Suite but not with the violence Wolfe had just described.

She wondered if the same person was responsible for Declan's death. If so, the culprit was obviously still searching for something in the actor's possessions.

But why kill Declan before getting what he or she was after?

13

Faith passed through the Great Hall Gallery, where the sun shone through the French doors and gilded the tile floor. It was another bright morning, chilly as expected in April, but she had reveled in the brisk walk from her cottage to the manor. Spring went right on dancing to the music of newly budded petals and birdsong, no matter what transpired in the world of men.

Yesterday's revelations, speculations, and fears could not be entirely eclipsed, yet nature's loyal and stubborn adherence to the rules inspired hope. Faith and her friends would get to the bottom of Declan's death—the why, the who—and absolve Brooke of suspicion. Faith straightened her shoulders and quickened her step.

She'd come to the manor early to touch base with Brooke, knowing her friend would already be preparing for the day. She took the stairs to the basement and entered the kitchen.

Brooke jumped at the sound of footsteps, and Faith saw that her face was pale, her eyes registering anxiety.

"Oh, it's you!" Brooke said with unmistakable relief.

"Are you okay?" Faith asked, then rebuked herself. Of course, Brooke wasn't all right. She'd been under suspicion by the police and probably convicted in the minds of some of the guests, giving credence to Brooke's fear that everyone would be gossiping about her.

"I'm okay," Brooke said. She let out her breath in a long sigh. "But I just feel so exposed. You know what I mean? Like everyone thinks I'm some kind of femme fatale."

Faith hugged her. "I'm sorry. This is awful for you, but we're going to get to the truth. It's going to be all right." *Easy for me to say,* she thought. *I'm not the one under suspicion.*

Brooke stepped away, then removed an apron from the rack and tied it around her waist. "I had the strangest feeling this morning. It felt like someone was watching me."

"What happened?" Faith asked.

"I parked a little farther away this morning than I usually do. I thought a walk might do me good. But I heard something in the bushes and began to feel uneasy. When I turned around, there was no one there."

Faith frowned. Someone had searched Declan's suite at the manor and had turned his apartment upside down looking for something. These events had to tie in with Declan's death. She knew there was danger afoot, but none of it made any sense.

"Maybe it was only my nerves," Brooke suggested. "I've been a basket case lately. I even forgot to feed Diva and Bling this morning. I was halfway down the street when I remembered and had to go back."

Laura poked her head into the kitchen. "Good morning." Her blonde hair waved softly around her face, and she was wearing a becoming green jacket.

"You're here early," Brooke commented.

"I thought I'd get a head start on my work," Laura said. "I was hoping to snag a cup of coffee on my way upstairs."

Smiling, Brooke poured a cup of coffee and handed it to Laura. "Thank you," she said.

"Did you go horseback riding yesterday?" Faith asked.

"Yes, it was fun. I haven't been on a horse in a long time. Colin showed me how to keep a better grip on the reins." Laura blushed. "Well, I'd better go. Thanks again, Brooke." She left as quickly as she'd arrived.

Laura seemed happy, and it no doubt had to do with Colin. Faith had no real reason to distrust the young man, but she'd feel better having a talk with him—the sooner the better.

As one of Brooke's assistants walked in and activity heightened for the day's culinary preparations, Faith left the kitchen and headed upstairs to the library. Her heart was heavy for Brooke. She longed for the whole mess over Declan's death to end, for them all to get back to their normal routines at the manor.

On the main floor, she was surprised to see Madeline climbing the staircase. She carefully carried a tray.

Faith called her name.

"Oh, good morning." Madeline smiled, her eyes shining with some inner merriment. Perhaps it was because she was on her own without her glum sister to spoil her delight.

It was easy to imagine Madeline as a sort of Pippi Longstocking who might just slide down the banister or skip the stairs two at a time. But another picture framed itself in Faith's mind—a woman dropping Marlene's rhinestone-studded watch into her tapestry bag.

"Is your sister ill this morning?" Faith asked, resting her hand on the railing in a subtle movement to detain the lady.

"It's only a headache," Madeline said, still smiling. "She gets them now and again if she eats too late at night." She gave Faith a conspiratorial wink. "I'm taking her some toast and her favorite white tea. It's called Silver Needle—*Bai Hao Yin Zhen*, actually. It's the purest of the white teas and has the most delicate flavor. White tea isn't rolled or oxidized, so it's lighter than green or black teas."

"I'm sorry about Corinna," Faith said. "Headaches can be so difficult. I hope she feels better soon."

"Thank you," Madeline said, then started to climb the stairs.

Faith needed to speak with Madeline. It was nothing but pure luck that she was alone this morning. "I wonder if you could spare me a moment. I promise we won't let the tea get cold. Or if it does, we'll make some fresh."

Madeline stopped and cocked her head like an inquisitive bird. "Well . . ."

"Let's go into the library," Faith suggested.

"I suppose I could for a few minutes," Madeline said.

"Please let me take the tray," Faith offered. She carried the tray and guided Madeline to the library, where she unlocked the door and ushered her inside.

"I can't get over how exquisite this library is," Madeline cooed, apparently not threatened or nervous about a requested audience. "I don't think it quite compares with anything I've ever experienced."

Faith set the tray down on the table. "We can talk over there." She led the way and motioned for Madeline to take the guest chair by her desk.

"Oh, what a gorgeous desk!" Madeline exclaimed, tracing a finger over the carving on the side nearest her. "I've never seen a cameo etched into a piece of furniture," she said excitedly, "or such ornate legs."

"It was part of the Jaxon family legacy," Faith said and leaned forward to capture Madeline's attention. "Dr. Morrissey," she began, using the formal address, "I wonder if you could help me."

Madeline's gaze drifted to the paperweight, which had mysteriously reappeared to grace the desk.

Faith glimpsed the first sign of anxiety in the woman's bright, birdlike eyes. Faith pointed to the fireplace. "Yesterday a friend of mine accidentally left her watch on the mantel over there."

Madeline remained silent.

"Marlene Russell, the assistant manager, took the watch off while we were talking because it was causing her wrist to itch." Faith paused, hoping for some explanation from Madeline. When none came, she went on. "The watch wasn't particularly valuable, but it's her favorite. I wondered if you might have seen it."

Madeline's face flushed, and she pushed back a wispy curl at her right temple. Then she appeared to brighten. "Once my mother had to give up wearing bracelets of any kind around her wrists because she broke out in an awful rash. And she'd never had one before. It was the strangest thing."

Faith watched her steadily, aware now that Madeline's defenses were weakening.

"Do you know that the single most common cause of dermatitis is an allergy to nickel, but it turns out—" Madeline stopped her lecture on metal allergies and glanced at the paperweight.

The door to the library opened, and Corinna marched in and strode toward them, brow furrowed, eyes wary. She was carrying Madeline's tapestry bag over the arm of her brown suit jacket. Her hair had been pulled back from her face, apparently in haste, for two thin gray strands strayed from their anchor at the base of her neck. She appeared ill.

Faith stood, an automatic reflex, as one might stand at attention or defer to royalty. "Your sister and I were just talking. She said you were not feeling well."

"Is there a problem?" Corinna asked severely.

Suddenly, Madeline burst into tears as though she were a child caught in mischief. "I'm sorry," she cried out. "I'm sorry."

Corinna pressed closer and rested a hand on her sister's shoulder. "You're overwrought. Come on. Get ahold of yourself."

Madeline's flow of tears abruptly stopped.

Despite her surprise, Faith heard herself say with an authority equal to Corinna's, "Should we determine what Madeline is sorry about?"

"She gets worked up emotionally," Corinna said without answering the question. "I'm sure she didn't mean to trouble you."

"She's not troubling me," Faith said. "But I believe she's distressed about what she's done." In the startled silence that followed, Faith turned to Madeline. "You did take the watch from the mantel, didn't you?"

Madeline stared down at her hands clasped in her lap and said nothing.

Corinna sat in the chair next to her sister and propped the tapestry bag on her lap. She regarded Faith for several seconds, then opened the bag and removed the watch. She passed it to Faith.

Madeline lifted her head and looked up through clouded eyes. She made a tent of her fingers and opened her mouth to speak, but no words came out.

"My sister doesn't know she's doing it," Corinna broke in. "She doesn't mean anything by it."

"I thought it was over," Madeline said, as though her sister had not spoken. She sighed deeply. "I never wanted to hurt anyone. I didn't want to steal anything. For a little while I was able to curb the impulse. But when I see something beautiful, I can't seem to help myself."

"*Kleptomania* is the proper term," Corinna said dully. "My sister cannot help but take the things that catch her eye. She doesn't do it for financial gain. It's an impulse."

Faith had never had any experience with the disorder or known anyone who suffered from it. And it was clear Madeline was suffering. Her heart ached for both sisters. "The purse hook, the gold pen, this paperweight," she said softly, picking up the keepsake from her desk. "You took them, didn't you?"

Madeline nodded.

"We've returned them all," Corinna said, glancing at Faith hopefully.

"I took my medication faithfully and went to therapy," Madeline said. "They were both working. I was certain I was cured, that it wouldn't happen again, but . . ." Her voice trailed off, and she spread her hands in a gesture of surrender.

"It all began again recently," Corinna said, shaking her head. "And just as Madeline was coming up for tenure at the university. It would be such a wonderful honor for her."

Silence hung in the air.

"Funny, isn't it?" Corinna went on. "I thought it was over after *he* was out of the picture. I thought no one would find out. I believed I could watch my sister, help her, and I did."

"Who do you mean?" Faith asked.

"Mr. Ames," Corinna confirmed, frowning. "He knew. When he found out five years ago, he threatened to reveal our secret and said the board would probably dismiss Madeline outright."

Faith almost gasped.

"But he didn't tell," Madeline insisted. "He never told anyone."

"Because he was compensated for his silence," Corinna snapped, the words splitting the tense air.

"Sister!" Madeline exclaimed.

"Yes, I paid him. I had to," Corinna said. "He would have ruined your chances, ruined your life."

Madeline appeared stunned and hurt. "How could you?"

"Oh, don't look at me like that. You don't understand the way things are." Corinna turned to Faith. "My sister sees the world through rose-colored glasses. It was only a few thousand dollars, and he kept quiet, but he always reminded me that he knew."

Madeline hung her head, sobbing.

"I'm so sorry about all this," Faith said. "You will need to seek treatment again, Madeline. You know that." She took a deep breath. "But I have to ask you. Did you have anything to do with what happened to Mr. Ames?"

Both sisters stared at her, their eyes wide. "No!" they blurted in unison.

Corinna stood, her face ashen. She paced a few feet and came back again. "We would never do something like that." Shame burned in two bright spots on her cheeks as she struggled to speak again. "I know I shouldn't have been glad when he died. I didn't want to feel relief, but I did."

Faith hadn't given serious consideration to the sisters being suspects, despite what she had seen and heard the night Declan had collapsed. But the police would probably have to be told about Madeline's kleptomania, and they would want to know where the sisters were the morning after when someone rummaged through Declan's belongings.

"What a mess I've created," Madeline said, wringing her hands. "And you, Sister, giving your money to him—all because of me!"

Corinna tucked a hand under Madeline's arm and helped her to her feet. "Come on. You need your rest, and I need my reflection." Recovering her control, she told Faith, "Once again, we are terribly sorry for everything. The items have all been returned, and there will be no more trouble. I can promise you that."

Faith turned Marlene's watch over and over in her hands, feeling a singular pity for the two sisters.

As though she'd been summoned, Marlene appeared in the doorway, a long burgundy scarf fluttering from her neck. She turned to watch the departing Morrissey sisters, then hurried toward Faith. Always on a mission, Marlene hardly ever strolled. "They seemed a bit grim. Is everything all right?"

"Perfect," Faith said, holding out the watch. Marlene didn't need to know the Morrissey sisters' secret quite yet. Wouldn't it be nice if it could remain buried a little longer? And if the fates were kind, Madeline's disorder could be cured once and for all and her reputation spared.

"Thank you," Marlene said as she took the watch. "I missed it. After all, I need to get where I'm going on time."

"How's the rash?" Faith asked.

"I think it was just nerves." Marlene grimaced as she worked to clasp her watch around her wrist. "Did you see Officer Laddy earlier?"

Faith shook her head. "Why?"

"I was just wondering because he was searching for one of the guests," Marlene said. "I thought he might have talked to you."

"No, I haven't seen him."

Marlene checked her watch. "I'd better get going." She hurried out of the room.

A few minutes later, Faith's cell phone buzzed. She picked up right away when she saw it was Eileen.

"Do you have a minute?" her aunt asked.

"Of course. Actually, I was wondering when you were going to call me like you promised," Faith teased.

"Very funny," Eileen said. "You know you can count on me."

"And your investigative skills," Faith added. "Did you find out anything about Declan?"

"It seems as though Declan's been busy at other things besides acting," Eileen answered. "In fact, he didn't take up this profession until recently."

"What do you mean?" Faith asked.

"Our Mark Twain impressionist has turned out to be something of a rogue," Eileen stated. "Or worse, he's been involved in some questionable business deals."

"Did you find any evidence of anything shady?"

"No, nothing I could pin down," Eileen admitted. "I wonder if Colin might help shed some light on his brother's activities."

"Maybe, but it's hard to get much out of Colin." Faith thought of Laura's smiling face and hoped that whatever Colin might know wouldn't hurt the vulnerable young woman.

"I keep mulling over what happened at Heatherstone College with Declan and Clement," Eileen said. "And how Clement might have wanted to take revenge on his old nemesis."

"Me too. Clement certainly had the motive. He's on the top of my suspect list." Faith thought of Corinna's confession that she had paid Declan to keep quiet about Madeline's kleptomania.

Had the actor been blackmailing Clement too?

14

Faith sat across from Chief Garris in his office at the police station. The sun shone in through the window behind his bald head and outlined his face. He was tall and imposing, even seated in his desk chair.

Garris checked his notes. "Miss Grimmell has been Mr. Kilpatrick's assistant for the past two years. Up until six months ago, she worked as an accountant at the private John P. Wellman Library in Boston, and she sometimes substituted for the librarian."

Faith had found that much out already through computer searches of her own, but she had made a special trip into town to see what else Garris might have uncovered. "Any past charges or anything in her record to indicate trouble between her and Declan?"

"Nothing official," the chief said, drawing his brows together. "Not even a parking ticket."

"What about her family? Does she have any brothers or sisters?" Faith asked, wondering if Edna had any siblings who might hold some kind of clue.

"Miss Grimmell was the only child of working-class parents," Garris answered.

"Do you have any idea how she met Declan?" Faith persisted.

"According to her statement, she met him at a meeting of the historical society. While she was still working at the library, she began assisting Mr. Kilpatrick part-time and arranged his appearances at various literary events. Then she moved to Hartford, where she rented an apartment."

"She may have been the last person to see Declan before his performance," Faith said thoughtfully. "Marlene delivered his dinner to his room, but Edna was right across the hall and could have put the drug in it before they came into the library together. Since it's a slow-acting drug, it might have taken an hour or more before doing its damage."

Garris nodded. "She's definitely a person of interest. But without a viable motive or a link to the drug, we don't have enough. We've already questioned her thoroughly. Her grief seems genuine, not only over Mr. Kilpatrick's death but over the loss of her job."

"What about Clement?" Faith asked. "Did you find anything out about him?"

The chief tapped his pen on the edge of his desk. "We followed your lead in the case of Mr. George, but there's no evidence of blackmail, at least not yet. We also can't trace the drug to him, and no one saw him near Mr. Kilpatrick's dinner tray or his suite that evening."

"What next?" Faith asked.

Garris leaned toward her, placing both hands on the desk between them. "We haven't exhausted our search yet. I know you're worried about Miss Milner, but we will get to the truth."

"Brooke is innocent," Faith stated. "She would never hurt anyone, let alone kill someone."

"Whatever is going on with those two unauthorized searches of Mr. Kilpatrick's suite and apartment may be connected to his death," the chief said, changing the subject. He peered at her closely. "There could be more trouble. I want you to be careful."

It was a caution he'd given her on more than one occasion. Faith knew he was only looking out for her, and she warmed to his fatherly concern. "I promise I'll be careful," she told him.

As Faith headed back to the library, she mulled over what she had learned and what remained a mystery.

With a few minutes remaining of her lunch hour, Faith stopped in the dining room to grab a sandwich.

She supposed there was no great hurry. Demands for her services in the library would be few since the guests were busily engaged in a seminar on the influence of Ralph Waldo Emerson and whether society and its institutions corrupted the purity of the individual, as the essayist and poet had proposed. It sounded like a heady topic destined to stimulate a discussion not quickly or easily settled.

Faith was surprised to see Colin sitting alone at a table in the far corner of the room with an empty plate and a can of soda. A book was open in front of him, but he seemed intent on something in the distance that only he could see. Colin wore jeans and a cable-knit sweater over a plaid shirt. He looked every bit the country veterinarian—another James Herriot.

After Faith took a sandwich and poured a cup of coffee, she ventured across the room. "Hello, Colin."

"Miss Newberry," he said, rising and accidentally closing his book in the process.

"Please call me Faith," she said with a smile, liking the fact that he had stood to greet her. *Manners are not totally defunct in the world,* she thought. "I'm sorry to disturb you." Perhaps he had been waiting to see Laura. They seemed to be gravitating toward each other. She hoped that was a good thing.

"Oh no, please," Colin said, obviously flustered. "You're not disturbing me. Would you like to sit down?" He gestured to a vacant chair at the table.

"Thank you," she said and slid into the seat across from him. "How are you?" She cringed at her thoughtless question.

"Fine."

"How was the horseback riding yesterday?" Faith asked as she stirred her coffee.

Colin appeared surprised. "How did you know?"

She smiled. "Laura mentioned it. She said it was a lot of fun."

"I'm afraid I talked her into it. I love to ride but seldom have time for it." Colin shrugged. "Right now, I seem to have nothing but time.

This waiting is a bummer." He picked up the can of soda and took a drink. "Miss Newberry," he began and seemed hesitant to say what was on his mind.

"Faith," she insisted, hoping to spur his confidence.

"How was my brother when he was here?" Colin finally asked. "I mean, what did you think of him?"

It was the first time she had heard him refer to Declan as his brother. She wondered how best to answer, not just with truth but with sensitivity. "He gave a remarkable presentation on Mark Twain. He had all of us engaged."

"Yes," he said with a frown, staring down at his long, graceful hands. "He always was a good teller of tales."

Faith couldn't help but notice that Colin's response sounded more like a complaint than a compliment. "He was friendly to the other guests." *Well, some of them.* "We are all so sorry about what happened." She rushed on, not wanting to lose this opportunity to talk with Colin about his brother. "Do you know if he took any medications? Maybe for pain or something else?"

"The police asked me that," Colin said in a dull voice. "I didn't even know he had a heart condition. Like I said, we weren't close. In fact, when he left home, I was glad. He made my mother's life miserable. She never knew where he was or when he'd be coming home. When I was a kid, I used to try to find ways to make up for things. I hated to see her cry, and I knew it was because of him."

"What about your father?" she asked quietly.

Colin toyed with the empty soda can, making small crackling noises as he dented it with his hands. "He wasn't around. He died when I was three. There was a fire in the factory where he worked. It was a substandard old building that was never brought up to code."

"I'm terribly sorry," Faith said.

"So, it was just me and Mom, and she was sick a lot. She died two years after I graduated from high school. I don't think she wanted to get well. Declan took off long before that, and he didn't call home much." Colin crushed the empty can in his hand.

Faith said nothing, the sound chilling her heart.

"He came to the funeral," Colin said with a hollow laugh. "But he didn't say a word to me. Just popped in and out like a deliveryman. He ruined my mom's life." He sat up straighter in his chair as though his own words had shocked him. "I'm sure you can see why I'm not all broken up over his death." He peered past her, and the little muscle in his temple flexed.

"I'm sorry," she said again, wishing there were better words. Yet he continued to sit and stare, and she felt he wanted to say something else. "Still, he was your brother," she said softly.

Colin drew in his breath and let it out slowly. "I guess I don't really know what that means."

Faith remained silent, waiting for him to continue.

"Declan hated being poor," Colin said. "And we were, though we had a roof over our heads and enough to eat. My parents came from County Cork in Ireland. They had big dreams, but they didn't live long enough to realize them. Declan was going after his oyster. Not just any oyster but one with the biggest pearl, and he didn't care how far he had to go to find it."

Faith recalled what Brooke had said about money being important to the Declan she had known. *He was absolutely fixated on money. That obsession turned me off more than anything else.* "But I understand that he did find his way into the university and later into acting school."

"Yes, it was surprising since he dropped out of high school. But he always had a yen to write. Mostly poetry. He talked about becoming another Patrick Kavanagh or Brendan Behan."

"Do you have any idea what led him to turn his focus to acting and doing impressions?" Faith asked.

"It beats me. But he's always been a fan of Mark Twain." Colin reached into an inside pocket in his sweater, drew out a folded square of paper, and held it up. "He's been dead to me for years, so why after all this time would he send me this?"

"But you said you and Declan hadn't spoken in years," she said in surprise.

"We haven't, but about two weeks ago I got a letter in the mail. This letter." He handed it to her. "I don't know how he found out where I lived. I know even less why he sent it."

Faith stared at the familiar broad, loopy script. It was the same handwriting in the letter to Brooke that pleaded for her love. It began without benefit of standard address but with a recognizable quote of Mark Twain's.

> "I was seldom able to see an opportunity until it had ceased to be one." Not knowing you as I ought is a lost opportunity, little brother, for after all, "The human race is a race of cowards; and I am not only marching in that procession but carrying a banner."

Faith glanced up at Colin after reading the first part of the letter, but the young man's eyes were fixed on something beyond her. She read on, amazed at the words that were largely Twain's.

> "It is good to begin life poor; it is good to begin life rich—these are wholesome; but to begin it prospectively rich! The man who has not experienced it cannot imagine the curse of it." Still, it is a curse I pass on—or a blessing, if carefully considered. Remember, "A man who carries a cat by the tail learns something he can learn in no other way."

The letter was signed simply D. K.

Faith reread the lines. An opportunity not taken, regret, self-reproach. Were these the words of a dying man to the brother he had neglected all his life? *Is this the suicide note after all?*

An almost giddy sense gripped her when she realized that Brooke need no longer be under suspicion. Nor anyone else for that matter. Declan must have taken the drug himself. He had written this letter two weeks before he died.

Faith struggled to keep her voice even. "Have you shown this to the police?" She already knew he hadn't because the letter was still in his possession. The police would have kept it. Why had he said nothing until now?

Colin shook his head. Then, taking the paper from her fingers, he set it down in front of him and carefully smoothed the folds. "Do you think he knew he was going to die?"

Faith searched his eyes, her mind whirling with thoughts too rapid to articulate. It certainly sounded like Declan had been preparing to die or go away. But how was it possible for him to ingest the drug and leave behind no trace of a container of any kind?

The kitchen at the manor and Brooke's pantry at home had been searched under a warrant as had Edna's suite. But someone had searched the Mark Twain Suite before the police got to it. Someone could have found the container and taken it. But why? Unless it would incriminate them. Or unless someone didn't want Declan to suffer the stigma of suicide.

"It's hard to believe he would do it," Colin said, almost in a whisper. "But it's equally hard to accept that someone deliberately ended his life."

Faith touched the letter on the table. "Whatever happened, you must give this to the police." He should have given it to them when they first questioned him, but then, it was a very personal letter.

He nodded but didn't move, the loopy scrawling still visible.

She thought about the letter. What had Declan meant by prospective riches being a curse? That his pursuit of money had been a mistake he needed to confess? And that quote—one of many Twain had written about cats—was he crediting Faja with his stroke of conscience? It was the strangest letter Faith had ever seen.

"You will talk to Chief Garris about this letter, won't you?" Faith persisted.

"This afternoon, I promise," Colin said, picking up the letter and returning it to his pocket. "Laura said she'd go with me." He colored slightly. "I told her about it, and she said I should talk to you. I want to thank you."

"No need." Glancing up, Faith saw Midge making a beeline toward them. Her friend carried her black vet bag with her initials imprinted in purple letters. With a reassuring touch on Colin's arm, Faith said, "We'll talk again."

Colin nodded, then left the dining room.

"You look like a woman on a mission," Faith said, arrested by the urgency she read on her friend's features.

"I'm headed to the kennels," Midge said. "I've been asked to check on the Amboys' dog, Buffy. Something about the toy poodle lying about and having no energy."

"Oh no. I hope their dog will be all right."

"Me too." Midge leaned in toward Faith. "But I have some news to share with you, and it's probably better that we talk outside." She glanced around, as though scanning the area for spies.

"The guests are at a seminar that will keep them busy all afternoon, so I should be able to break away for a little while," Faith said. "Let me grab my jacket."

"Good," Midge said. "Then I can fill you in."

They stopped in the library for Faith's jacket, then started walking toward the kennels and stables.

"Were you talking to Declan's kid brother?" Midge asked, tossing back strands of blonde hair that blew across her face in the spring wind.

"Yes, and it was quite illuminating. He told me he received a letter from Declan two weeks before he died." Faith highlighted the communication's cryptic contents. "It may be the suicide note."

"But why would Declan decide to do away with himself here in front of everybody?" Midge said. "And why wasn't some evidence found? Crazy break-ins aside, I'm not buying it."

"It's definitely puzzling," Faith agreed. "What did you want to tell me?"

Midge swung her bag to the other arm. "Remember I told you about my cousin who's a genealogy genius—you know, finding long-lost relatives and that sort of thing?"

Faith nodded as she recalled Midge's offer to reach out to her cousin when they were discussing the case at their book club meeting.

"Well, she called me this morning," Midge continued. "And she gave me some interesting information about that cowboy professor."

"What did she say about Clement?"

"He has a sister in New Britain," Midge replied. "Guess what business the sister's husband is in."

"I have no idea."

"He owns an independent pharmacy in New Britain. It's only about an hour away from Cornwall, where Clement lives." Midge pursed her pink lips. "If the professor wanted to get his hands on a certain drug, who do you suppose would be his go-to guy?"

"But that would be illegal," Faith said, blurting out her first thought.

"So is murder."

Faith swallowed. Clement wouldn't have offered this information to the police during his statement and questioning. Why would he? It was difficult to imagine that the erudite, well-spoken gentleman cowboy would stoop to such tactics, even though he had good reason to view Declan as an enemy. But of course, erudite, well-spoken gentlemen had been known to commit murder.

"I suppose we have to add possible means to the equation where Clement is concerned," Faith admitted. "But it doesn't necessarily mean anything."

"Speaking of the professor, look there." Midge pointed toward the stable, surrounded by white rail fencing. In the corral, the gorgeous bay horse stood perfectly still as Clement brushed his gleaming flank.

The big man sporting a white Stetson seemed to be talking to his horse. Beau, if Faith remembered right. *Do the good guys really wear white hats?*

"Let's have a chat with him," Faith suggested. "Maybe he'll admit something or at least let something slip."

"Do you think that's wise?" Midge asked. "We might be conversing with a killer."

"Come on," Faith said, tugging lightly on Midge's sleeve. "He has no reason to worry about us."

"I guess not," Midge conceded, "but I'll bet he won't exactly be tickled to learn we know about his brother-in-law's pharmacy in New Britain."

"Morning, ladies," Clement said to them when they climbed over the rail. "Beautiful day."

Faith greeted him with a smile.

He nodded and tipped his hat briefly. "You have some fine horses here at the manor. Are you going out on the trail too?"

"Not me," Midge said. "I treat their ailments, but I make it a practice to stay off their backs."

Faith glanced around and saw two other guests saddling horses. If she went riding, she wouldn't be alone with Clement, but there could be an opportunity for conversation. "Well," she said, considering, "I might go for a short ride. That is, if Samuel can find me a not-too-frisky mount this morning."

"I'd be honored to accompany you—not that you need any assistance, I'm sure," Clement said. Then he turned back to his horse, wielding the brush with a muscular arm.

While Clement's back was turned, Midge nudged Faith and whispered, "Don't ride with him. He could be dangerous."

"You go along and tend to the Amboys' poodle. I'll be back." Faith walked to the stable door and away from the warning in Midge's green eyes. "Ah, there's Samuel now."

15

"Miguel is bringing Belle for you," Samuel said. The head groom hefted a saddle over a stall rail and shrugged off his gloves. "I believe you've ridden her before. She's a steady old girl."

Belle was a Missouri Fox Trotter, a sure-footed breed used mainly for trail riding and ranch work. She had a black coat with a mane and tail of the same color, sloped shoulders, a short back, and sturdy legs, and her ambling gait provided a smooth ride.

"Sounds good," Faith said. "I rode Avalanche once, and he was as devastating as his name."

Samuel laughed, then gestured to a brawny man in his thirties with straight black hair who was leading the horse over to them. "Here they are."

It suddenly occurred to Faith that Miguel, the new hand, didn't look anything like the man she had glimpsed a few days earlier when she had visited the stables with Eileen. He'd been of medium height and slight build, but Miguel was shorter and a good thirty pounds heavier.

As Faith watched Miguel prepare Belle for the trail, she tried unsuccessfully to match the stranger's description with one of the guests at the manor.

"All set, ma'am," Miguel said, ending her reverie. He helped her mount and led the horse out into the corral, where Clement was waiting with the other riders.

The wrangler recited the obligatory rules of the trail, and the riders were off with Faith and Clement at the rear of the line.

When the trail widened, Clement drew Beau up alongside Belle. "Great day for a ride," he said. Holding the reins easily in one hand, he tipped his hat with the other.

"It's lovely," Faith agreed, but she concentrated on gripping the reins with the proper amount of tension and adjusting to the saddle. "I'm a little rusty," she admitted.

"No problem. I guess a busy librarian like yourself doesn't have much time for leisure."

"Oh, I take time for what's important to me," she said. There was a considerable gap between them and the other riders, for which she was alternately grateful and apprehensive. The purpose for this ride wasn't leisure but to see what made this man tick and whether he had three days ago managed to dispatch his nemesis to his eternal reward.

Clement led his horse steadily forward through forest trails and greening hills. For a mile or more, they rode without speaking as they traveled through the fragrant countryside blossoming with new life.

"I was sorry to miss your lecture on Bret Harte," Faith said, trying to stimulate conversation. "He's a wonderful American author—despite what Mark Twain had to say about him."

Clement didn't respond. He simply stared straight ahead.

"It's strange," she continued, "because they were friends—even worked together—until something happened and they became bitter enemies. I read that Twain wrote to the president to try to stop Harte from being offered a diplomatic post overseas."

"You're remarkably well-read on the subject," Clement commented, briefly allowing Beau to drift to the side of the trail, where lush grass grew.

"I thought it was important to brush up on the latest scholarship for this particular retreat," Faith said. "It's sad when friends become enemies. But I suppose things like that happen among colleagues."

Clement turned to look at her directly. "Is this about two American classic authors? Or are you asking about my relationship with Declan Ames?"

"I must admit that I am curious. I felt terrible about the way he treated you that first night when we met in the library." When he made no response, she continued. "You were at Heatherstone when you met Declan Ames, weren't you? I suppose I should say Declan Kilpatrick. He didn't go by a stage name back then."

"No, he was just an arrogant student who thought he knew more than all his teachers put together." Clement spurred his horse back onto the main trail with an angry jerk of the reins. "But that plagiarism charge was never proven."

She quickly drew alongside him, eliciting a complaining snort from Belle. "But you left the college ten years ago when they wouldn't renew your contract."

"Your information is accurate," he said with something approaching a sneer. "You've been busy trying to clear your friend's name by digging into my affairs. But what you really want to know is if I hated Declan enough to kill him."

Faith remained silent.

"The answer is yes. I found the man detestable, but I didn't kill him." Clement straightened in the saddle. "And I think I've answered enough questions. I've had to put up with the police asking questions—no doubt because of a tip from you about my history with the dearly departed. But I shouldn't have to suffer an interrogation from a nosy librarian."

"Do you get over to New Britain very often?" Faith asked. "Perhaps to your brother-in-law's pharmacy?"

Clement's face went ashen beneath his sportsman's tan, and he glared at her for a long moment. "I've had enough of the trail for one day. Good afternoon to you." He wheeled around, then took off at a gallop, leaving her staring after him.

When Faith got back to the stable after rejoining the rest of the group, Clement had gone, leaving his horse with Samuel.

Midge, however, was waiting, pacing back and forth outside the fence. "You really had me worried. I saw Clement come back alone, and he didn't look happy."

"I may have made an enemy today," Faith said. "But I know I struck a nerve by mentioning his brother-in-law's pharmacy in New Britain."

"You shouldn't have gone off with him. I called Wolfe, by the way, and told him about Clement's connection to the pharmacy." Midge took Faith's arm. "He'll make sure Chief Garris knows."

"That will really make Clement's day." Faith sighed. She briefly sketched in the short conversation she'd had with Clement.

"Do you think he murdered Declan?" Midge asked.

"I don't know," Faith answered. "I can't quite see him doing something like that after all this time."

"Maybe Declan made a more recent threat or blackmailed him," Midge suggested.

"Maybe," Faith echoed. She pushed away the confusing thoughts about Clement and changed the subject. "How's the toy poodle doing?"

"Buffy's fine now. She ingested a custard doughnut. It had a thin chocolate icing, but it was enough to make her sick. I gave Mr. and Mrs. Amboy the speech about how chocolate can be deadly. I hope they watch her more carefully from now on." She cocked her head at Faith. "Are you all right?"

Faith realized that she hadn't been giving Midge her complete attention. "Do you remember the other day when we walked to the kennels and saw Clement brushing his horse?"

Midge nodded.

"After you left to check on the horses, Eileen and I saw a man we didn't recognize. It was just a glimpse, and we couldn't see his face. I assumed it was the new hand Samuel had hired."

Midge waited, curiosity sparking in her eyes.

"Well, it's not. The new hire is a man named Miguel. He's short and brawny, and he doesn't look anything like the guy we saw."

"Do you think he was one of the guests?"

"I don't believe so." Faith hurried to keep pace with Midge, knowing she'd delayed her friend from getting back to work. "What if the person who slipped the drug to Declan wasn't one of the manor guests? What if it was someone completely unknown to us who came in from the outside?"

"Like the stranger at the stable?" Midge asked.

Faith shrugged. "Maybe." Something about the way he moved was familiar, though. She shivered as she remembered Brooke's odd feeling of being watched.

"But why would this person stick around after murdering Declan?" Midge asked.

"What if there was something he wanted and thought Declan had in his possession?" Faith paused, a new thought occurring to her. "Maybe even Colin—"

"His kid brother?" Midge exclaimed. "But he didn't get into town until the day after Declan died."

"Do we know for sure that he was in Boston when the police contacted him? Maybe they called his cell. What if he was near Lighthouse Bay? Or perhaps he'd been here all along?" The idea shocked her even as she articulated it. *Is it possible that fine, sensitive young man killed his own brother?*

"But what about the letter Colin showed you?" Midge argued.

"It could have been a fake." Everything in Faith wanted to believe it was genuine. It was so like the one Brooke had received. But it could have been contrived, and the police probably had not yet authenticated the writing as Declan's. "Oh, it's all such a confusing muddle."

"You can say that again." Midge grabbed Faith's arm and hugged it tight to her own as they walked the rest of the way to the manor.

Wolfe entered the library shortly after Faith returned from the stable. He halted at her desk and asked, "Are you all right?"

"I'm fine," she said.

He glanced around to see if any guests were in the near vicinity. "Midge phoned to say you were out riding with Professor George." His eyes clouded with what she knew was concern.

"I hope Midge told you that we were with several others on the trail," Faith said. "There was nothing to worry about."

"But we don't know what that man is capable of," Wolfe protested. "Why did you go?"

"I needed to sound him out after I heard that his brother-in-law owns a pharmacy in New Britain."

Wolfe sat down in the chair by her desk and leaned toward her. "The police could have done that. They will do that." He gazed at her intently. "I don't want you taking any chances. I don't want you getting hurt."

Faith melted under his concerned scrutiny and hurried to reassure him. She shared what she learned from Clement and her worry about an outsider on the manor's grounds. "Eileen and I saw a man around the stables the day Declan died. I caught only a glimpse of him, but I could tell he was medium height with a slight build. I assumed he was the new hand Samuel had hired, but it wasn't Miguel."

"The man you described doesn't sound like any of our guests," Wolfe said. "Could you see his face at all?"

"No, and I couldn't see the color of his hair because he wore a dark cap," Faith replied, then told him about Brooke's sense of being watched. "I know she's under a great deal of stress, but I'm still concerned."

"We'll be on guard," Wolfe said. "But promise me—no, I won't exact a promise I know you won't keep. But please don't take unnecessary risks. You're far too important to all of us." He held her gaze tenderly for a long moment.

When two guests entered the library, Wolfe got up. "I'll talk to you later," he said and left the room.

The rest of the afternoon passed quickly. When the last guest had left the library, Faith locked the door and went home to a supper of braised salmon and asparagus spears. It was good to enjoy the undemanding company of Watson and Faja after a day of unsettling events and jangled nerves. Her lower back was protesting the day's activities too.

"Your mistress isn't used to the saddle," she said to Watson.

The cat didn't glance up as he nibbled precious bits of salmon she had added to his kibble.

Faja, who had been huddling over her bowl of food that was also mixed with Faith's leftovers, mewed what Faith interpreted as a feline thank-you.

"I know you've missed going to the library with me," she told Watson, bending to pat his silky head.

Faith had kept Faja inside for the past two days since she'd brought the cat to the cottage. The Ragdoll was unused to her new surroundings, and Faith was afraid the cat might run off. As far as she knew, Watson had stayed inside with Faja and hadn't pulled one of his famous disappearing tricks.

She eased down on the couch and watched Faja and Watson laboriously cleaning themselves in the last rays of sunlight coming in the living room. She closed her eyes, treasuring Wolfe's expression of caring, though she regretted causing him to worry.

After a few moments of reverie, she decided to turn on the television to get the evening news. But as she picked up the remote, she heard a car approaching. She glanced out the window. Laura and Colin were coming up the walk.

Faith hurried to the door and opened it before they could knock.

"We're sorry to bother you at home," Laura began, her eyes bright. She glanced at Colin shyly but with recognizable infatuation. "Colin and I were talking about his brother's cat, and he'd like to see her. I told him you were taking care of her temporarily."

"I hope it's not a terrible imposition." Colin bowed slightly, and a lock of his hair fell over his forehead. "After what Declan wrote in the letter . . ." His voice trailed off. He was silent for a moment before continuing. "I did take the letter to the police headquarters."

Faith searched the faces of her young visitors, recalling as she stood in the doorway what Declan had written: *"A man who carries a cat by the tail learns something he can learn in no other way."* It was natural for Colin to be curious if his brother credited his pet with a kind of repentance. Or simply curious because as a veterinarian he loved animals.

"Of course you're not imposing," Faith said. "Come in, you two. Would you like a cold drink or a cup of coffee?"

"We've just had dinner," Laura said, readjusting the strap of her purse on her shoulder. "Please don't go to any trouble."

The two cats paused in their ablutions and blinked at the visitors, who sat down at opposite ends of the couch.

"Laura said you had a very clever tuxedo cat," Colin said as he regarded Watson. "He's a beautiful specimen. What happened to his tail?"

Faith told him the story of finding Watson on the street and how his bobbed tail was the result of an injury when he was a kitten.

Faja stopped washing her face and sat elegantly with her bushy tail curled around her, gazing at Colin.

"This is Faja," Faith said. "I was going to take her to the kennels, but when I saw her in a cage in Declan's suite, I decided she'd have more freedom here at my cottage."

"I love your house," Laura said. "It's so quaint and full of character. I like how bright and airy everything feels. And if I could have a bay window like this, I'd think I was in absolute heaven."

Faja padded over to the couch, daintily sniffing Colin's feet as Watson jumped onto the back of Faith's chair and nestled close to her shoulder.

"I'm sure she won't mind if you pick her up," Faith said, indicating the curious Faja. "She likes to be petted and seems to make herself at home quickly."

Colin narrowed his eyes, appearing to study the gaudy, jeweled collar around Faja's neck.

Faja leaped up suddenly into the man's lap and gave an endearing little mew.

"She's a little heartbreaker, isn't she?" Faith said, laughing.

"Why, you're all fur," Colin said as he stroked the docile animal. "Fur and collar. And you're a lot heavier than you look." He ran his fingers over the cheap plastic gems. "That's the biggest collar I've ever seen. You'd think she was Cleopatra's royal cat."

"She seems to be used to it," Faith said.

"What will happen to her now that Declan's gone?" Colin asked quietly as he patted Faja with his long, graceful hands.

Faith had been struck by Colin's hands when they'd sat at dinner the night he'd arrived and earlier that day when he'd shown her Declan's letter. They were hands that might play the violin or paint exquisite pictures. *Or use his medical knowledge to poison his brother's dinner?*

Colin was next of kin, and he could have the cat if he wanted her. But for now, things were too unsettled to start dispatching Declan's belongings. "I understand that Miss Grimmell used to take care of Faja occasionally," she said hesitantly. "But she doesn't seem inclined to take her on, especially since she's highly allergic to cats."

Colin's expression gave nothing away, but Faith could see the muscles in his jaw tense.

She recalled Edna's scornful words: *I've been the one to see to his affairs. There's no one else to handle things except me. You can bet that so-called brother of his won't lift a finger.*

"Is Faja healthy?" Colin asked. "Does she have a good appetite?" He examined her, massaging the cat's furry neck and shoulders.

"Yes, Faja has been fine, and she has a healthy appetite," Faith answered. "Edna thought she had swallowed something, and our vet was called, but it turned out to be a false alarm."

She thought about Faja running into the room followed by a distraught Edna. Moments later, Declan had fiercely decried his assistant's ineptness and demanded to know who had stolen the cat's collar.

"That's great to hear." Colin gently set Faja down on the floor and stood. "We've taken up enough of your time. We'll get out of your way."

"It's no problem," Faith said.

"Thank you for letting me see Faja." Colin stared down at the cat at his feet. "She must be something special if she made my brother reevaluate his life. Too little too late," he muttered. He turned to Laura. "Are you ready?"

Laura nodded. She got up and grabbed her purse.

Faith watched them head toward the old sedan parked in her driveway. Laura was talking, gazing up at the handsome young man who had claimed her attention.

But Colin remained focused on the path ahead.

Faith shivered. Who was he really? Did he truly deserve Laura's admiration?

16

A bleak sun penetrated flinty clouds four days after Declan Ames Kilpatrick had collapsed in the library. The retreat was fast coming to an end—without closure on what had happened to the actor.

Faith got up with a little encouragement from two hungry cats who didn't believe in sleeping in, even on a Saturday.

She laughed. "All right, I'm up, but if it weren't for the fact that Brooke is coming by for pancakes, you two would be in trouble."

Close on her heels, Watson and Faja followed her into the kitchen, weaving in and out at her feet and purring in anticipation. They paced to their empty food bowls and back to where she stood at the sink.

Faith stared out at the grim weather. Rain was predicted—the April showers that would bring May flowers. The day would be gloomy. The good news was that Colin's letter from his brother might take the pressure off Brooke and the other suspects. But she wondered how suicide could really spell good news.

She recalled Declan's lines, incorporated into a Mark Twain quote, that had been so startling: *Not knowing you as I ought is a lost opportunity, little brother, for after all, "The human race is a race of cowards; and I am not only marching in that procession but carrying a banner."*

Had Declan been expressing regrets as he contemplated leaving the world? But if he had taken the lethal dose of Ziophaine, where had he disposed of the bottle? The police had not found any outward evidence of the drug in his suite or anywhere else in the manor.

And why had Declan's home as well as his temporary residence at the manor been ransacked? Faith thought the break-ins had to be connected to his death, but she didn't know how.

Watson butted his head against her ankle. It was a less-than-subtle reminder that she had yet to provide his breakfast.

Faith opened the cupboard, then filled their bowls.

Faja made a beeline to her breakfast, and Watson calmly took his time as though he wasn't in the least bit hungry, thank you very much.

She suspected that Watson would miss the docile Ragdoll when a permanent home was found for her. To all outward appearances, the two cats had become remarkably comfortable together.

The curious quote contained in Declan's letter drifted through her mind again: *"A man who carries a cat by the tail learns something he can learn in no other way."*

What had Declan learned? Or was there some secret the cat had yet to divulge?

Hearing a car approach, she went to the front door to welcome Brooke. Guests at the manor were to be served a continental breakfast, and the chef had the rare morning off.

Brooke waved as she got out of her Mazda. She was wearing designer jeans and a mint-green top with lace trim at the neck and sleeves. Her short hair curled softly around her face like a pale cloud. The effect was soft femininity and vulnerability.

"Good Saturday morning," Faith said as she ushered her friend inside. "Come in out of the rain."

"Just a light mist right now," Brooke said, tossing her shoulder bag on the nearest chair. "How come I don't smell pancakes?"

"Any good chef knows you don't cook pancakes until you see the whites of your guest's eyes," Faith teased.

"Well, now you see them." Brooke leaned forward and opened her eyes wide.

Faith noticed small worry lines etched between Brooke's eyebrows. The week had been a hard one for her.

Faith led Brooke into the kitchen, then lit the burner under her frying pan.

The two cats glanced up at Brooke from their side-by-side bowls.

"They seem chummy," Brooke commented. She sat down at the table, which Faith had set the night before with her Delft Blue china and a vase of daffodils in the center.

"They've had a few days to get acquainted, and they're doing surprisingly well," Faith said, mixing the batter. "I've kept Faja inside for now. I don't want her to be confused by her new surroundings and run off."

"I'm glad they're getting along."

After pouring the batter into the pan, Faith turned to study her friend's pale features. "Is Diva doing okay after that little upset?"

"She's fine," Brooke said with a sigh. "Bling, on the other hand, has been going around in circles so fast it makes my head spin. I guess she can't decide which direction to take." She smiled weakly.

Brooke often projected her own emotions onto her fish without realizing it. And there was no question that Brooke was having a rough time.

Faith flipped the pancakes over in the pan. "Well, I heard something that may be a game changer. Colin got a letter from Declan two weeks ago and just told us about it yesterday."

"I know," Brooke said.

"How did you find out?"

"Laura told me about it before I left last night." Brooke frowned. "I should be relieved if Declan killed himself. But I keep thinking that if I hadn't turned him down like I did, then maybe he wouldn't have done it."

Faith put her arm across Brooke's shoulders. "Get that idea out of your head right now. You are not responsible for what he did."

"I wish I had known that he was so troubled," Brooke insisted. "Perhaps I could have done something to help."

Faith transferred the pancakes to a serving plate. "You couldn't have known that." She set the plate on the table and sat down across from her friend. "A lot of time has passed since you knew him. Whatever transpired has nothing to do with you."

"I just can't imagine that he would take his own life," Brooke said sadly.

"There are still so many unanswered questions about what happened that night. The investigation isn't over." Faith handed Brooke a bottle of blueberry syrup. "Made from lowbush blueberries in Maine. It's so good."

Brooke poured syrup over a steaming pancake but made no move to pick up her fork. She scrunched up her forehead. "So, the police think someone else might have killed Declan, but I'm still suspect number one?"

"I'm not sure you were ever number one on the list," Faith answered. "Edna had more opportunity, and Clement had a strong motive. Even the Morrissey sisters had more reason to want Declan dead."

Brooke remained silent.

Faith poured blueberry syrup over her pancake. "Also, the police haven't ruled out the possibility that someone completely unknown to us could be involved. And the break-ins at the Mark Twain Suite and at Declan's apartment in Hartford have to be connected somehow." *But how?*

Brooke toyed with her food, twirling a chunk of pancake around in the syrup. She glanced up at Faith, then back down at her plate, as though she wanted to say something and wasn't sure how. Finally, she set her fork down and clasped her hands in her lap. "Remember when I told you that I felt someone watching me when I was walking to my car?"

Faith nodded.

"Last night, when Laura was telling me about Colin's letter, we were both startled by a noise in the bushes behind us."

Both, Faith thought. *Not just Brooke but Laura too.* "Where were you?"

"We were walking to the parking lot after work. Laura needed a ride home, and we sat down by the Peter Pan fountain for a few minutes. It was such a pretty day and only just beginning to get dark. Laura said she wanted to tell me something."

Faith pictured the whimsical fountain dedicated to perpetual life. The garden feature near the maze was nicely secluded with a cedar hedge surrounding it. It was too early in the season for the fountain to be filled with water, but it was still beautiful with its cherubic figures around the base and atop the center pole.

"That's when Laura told me that Colin confided in her about the letter." Brooke raised an eyebrow. "She's been distracted and dreamy since he arrived. You know Laura. But she has a remarkable memory. I think she recalled every sentence of that strange letter—even that funny bit about learning something important from a cat."

Faith waited, her breakfast going cold on her plate. "And that's when you heard something in the bushes?"

"Laura looked around, but she didn't see anything." Brooke shrugged. "It was probably a squirrel or maybe one of the guests walking a pet. Or it could have been Watson prowling around back there."

"What did you do then?"

"It was spooky enough that we got back on the lighted path and headed for my car." Brooke took a deep breath. "You don't suppose there really is someone lurking around and watching, do you?"

Faith tamped down her instant apprehension. She had seen a man around the stables when she and Eileen had walked there. Wolfe hadn't discounted it when she told him about it and said they would be vigilant. She hesitated, not wanting to worry Brooke even more. "I suppose it could have been one of the police officers," she said calmly. "We know they're keeping an eye on things at the manor."

But Faith realized that if it had been someone from the police department, the officer would have announced his or her presence. A cop wouldn't have frightened guests out of their wits.

Brooke said nothing, but the wrinkles in her forehead deepened.

"Just the same, stay away from secluded places," Faith said, then attempted to lighten the mood. "Now, if you don't eat that pancake, I'm going to think my favorite chef doesn't like my cooking."

After Brooke left the cottage, Faith got ready for work. On her way out the door, she petted Watson and Faja and gave them a few tunaroons. "Be good, you two. I'll be back soon."

Visitors to the library were few, which gave Faith some time to spend at the computer. And to puzzle further over Declan's death and how the break-ins might be related. Someone was searching for something, and that something was obviously connected to the actor.

Her cell phone vibrated in her pocket. She brightened to see Eileen's name on the screen. She always felt better when she talked to her aunt. She had a way of spreading peace.

"Hi, honey. Are you busy?" As usual, Eileen sounded cheerful and eager, but there was a new urgency to her voice.

"No, the library is quiet at the moment," Faith replied. "Brooke had the morning off, and we had breakfast together."

"Oh, good. How is she?"

"I think she's doing all right under the circumstances, but she's still pretty nervous, feels like she's being watched." Faith swallowed, thinking about what Brooke had experienced while she and Laura were talking at the Peter Pan fountain.

"Not surprising," Eileen said. She paused, then continued with her typical enthusiasm. "You know I've been digging into the details of Declan's background."

"What did you find?" Faith asked.

"About six months ago, Declan and Edna left Boston within a week of each other," Eileen announced.

"But I thought Declan was in Hartford when he and Edna met up and she began arranging his appearances," Faith said. "Declan was involved in theater work in Boston, but he maintained his Hartford connection."

"Edna suddenly quit her job at the John P. Wellman Library in Boston," Eileen said. "Do you know that she didn't even pick up her last paycheck before leaving the city?"

"Well, we know she's pretty temperamental," Faith said. "I've seen so many sides to her since she's been here. Maybe someone rubbed her the wrong way at the library, and she just decided she'd had enough."

"Maybe. But suppose there was a connection to Boston and to Edna's abrupt departure from the library," Eileen suggested. "I think we need to keep searching. I'm sure the police are checking, but we can't leave any stone unturned."

"You're right, but I've been focused on Declan's connection to Clement."

"You shouldn't have gone off riding with him, you know," Eileen scolded. She sighed, perhaps knowing she'd never be able to curb her niece's investigating nerve. Which, Faith realized, was very much like hers.

Eager to change the subject, Faith offered, "I've got some time today now. Most of the guests are busy with a seminar on Oliver Wendell Holmes. I'll narrow the Boston search to recent events and see if anything turns up."

"Sounds good," Eileen said. "You take care of yourself."

"I promise. I'll be in touch." Faith clicked off and pulled up a list of Boston news outlets on her computer.

Before she could begin her search, Corinna came into the library, her light step a stark contrast to her usual stiff demeanor. She smiled as she approached Faith's desk.

Faith was surprised by Corinna's unusual behavior and the fact that she was unaccompanied by the charming Madeline.

Corinna sat down across from Faith. "I wanted you to know that we've made an appointment for next week. My sister is quite willing, anxious even, to get back into therapy. We're both grateful to you for your kindness."

"That's wonderful news," Faith said, reaching across the desk to touch Corinna's hand. "It's been a pleasure to have you here at the manor, and I wish you both the very best."

"Thank you." Corinna smiled again, then got up and left the library.

Faith watched her go, grateful that calamity had been averted and that the precocious and highly gifted Madeline Morrissey would find relief from the compulsion that drove her.

She turned back to the computer, willing herself to focus on the media outlets she wanted to explore. There were so many websites, archived news reports, and updates. Was there really a needle in any of those haystacks?

A full hour passed with only an occasional guest needing her assistance. Faith perused the usual reports of events in the burgeoning city of Boston—homicides, explosions, train wrecks, burglaries, strikes, home invasions, and the like. None of them mentioned Declan Kilpatrick or any other familiar name.

Faith zeroed in on the most recent year, checking headlines in major Boston newspapers.

Then a headline caught her attention. A quarter of a million dollars' worth of cut diamonds had been stolen from a holding company on Boston's southwest side. Two men, possibly three, had been involved and gotten away without a trace in the midnight caper. The report was dated a little over six months ago.

Faith pulled up a map of Boston and checked the coordinates and location of landmarks in the city. When she spotted the John P. Wellman Library, she felt a spark of excitement. That was the private library where Edna had been employed.

She read on to discover that the library was within walking distance of the burglary site. According to the report, no one at the library had seen any suspicious activity or persons in the area. Subsequent reports on the theft indicated that no arrests had been made and the jewels had not been recovered.

When Marlene appeared at the library door, Faith saved the page and exited the site reluctantly. It was hardly anything to get excited about anyway. The heist had nothing to do with Wellman, other than the fact that it had occurred near the library. But it would be interesting to know if Edna had been on duty when the investigators went to the library seeking information.

Since it was Saturday, the assistant manager had dressed down a little. She wore gray slacks, a black silk blouse without a suit jacket, and low-heeled shoes that rendered her considerably shorter. "Have things been pretty quiet around here today?" she asked, sitting down next to Faith's desk.

"Actually, yes. Just the occasional drop-in or two." Faith studied Marlene's drawn features. She looked exhausted. "Is everything all right?"

Marlene narrowed her eyes. "Is *anything* all right?" she responded testily. "Police coming and going and everyone wanting to know the latest developments in the investigation." She grimaced. "Professor George just gave me a piece of his mind—a piece I think belongs to you. The police questioned him again after getting that tip about his brother-in-law's pharmacy in New Britain."

"As they should," Faith said. "Clement has a strong motive and the means to cause Declan's death. It was Midge's cousin who found the connection. I merely tested his reaction to the information when we went riding. I could tell the news got to him. So, if there's a piece of his mind up for grabs, it probably does belong to me."

Suddenly, the library door opened, and Edna headed straight for Marlene, her brows a straight line above her glasses. Her arms swung at her sides, and her Cuban heels pounded the floor. "What have you done with Faja?" she demanded, stopping directly in front of the assistant manager.

Marlene rose, forcing Edna to take a step back. "Excuse me?"

Edna's face flushed. Two bright spots bloomed on her cheeks. "I went to see her at the kennels, but she wasn't there." She whipped out a lace-edged handkerchief and touched it to her red nose. "Mr. Ames trusted me to take care of his beloved pet, and you said she'd be at the kennels."

Interesting, Faith thought. *Edna waited three days to check on Declan's beloved pet.*

"Please calm down," Marlene said sharply.

"Calm down! Calm down!" the woman ranted. "Mr. Ames is dead, and now his dearest possession is gone. You promised to look after her." She raised her arms as though to ward off blows, the handkerchief waving. "How much more do I have to take?"

"Don't worry," Marlene said calmly. "Faja is doing well."

Edna put the handkerchief to her nose and blew loudly. "Where is she? Who is taking care of her?"

"She is being cared for by a member of our staff," Marlene said without glancing at Faith. "There's no need for concern."

"Faja is staying at my cottage," Faith said, breaking into the conversation. "We thought she would be happier there than in one of the kennels with a lot of barking dogs. I assure you she's well-fed and content."

"You?" Edna said. "She's with you? But you own the cat that attacked her."

"Faja and Watson are getting along just fine," Faith said evenly.

Edna's stormy eyes flashed from Faith to Marlene and back again. "Well, you can understand my concern when I didn't find her, and no one at the kennel knew anything."

Faith had talked to Annie, but she must have been out when Edna went searching for Faja.

"It's such a relief to know she's all right." Edna sniffed the air dramatically. "Poor Faja. Poor lost kitty without her cherished master. It would be such a comfort to have Faja with me now that Mr. Ames is gone."

A pregnant pause elapsed before Marlene said in a voice that brooked no argument, "I do not think it would be wise to move her at this time. We pledged responsibility for Mr. Ames's safety and that of his possessions when he joined the retreat."

"And a pretty mess you've made of that!" Edna spouted, her tears obviously forgotten.

Marlene's jaw tightened, but her response was measured and controlled. "Until the investigation is over or a next of kin assumes responsibility, we will continue to care for his cat."

"All right," Edna conceded. "I've been so upset since Mr. Ames passed. I'm sorry that I took it out on you." She put the lace-trimmed handkerchief to her nose once again.

Faith couldn't help but feel sorry for Edna. She was pretty sure the woman viewed Declan as much more than a boss or even a friend. And despite her allergy to cats, she had faithfully cared for his pet.

"You're welcome to come by the cottage anytime," Faith offered. "I'm sure Faja would be glad to see you, and you can be assured that she's all right."

Edna seemed almost penitent as she dabbed at her eyes with her handkerchief. "Mr. Ames would want me to thank you." She gave a deep sigh and walked away.

17

The cat climbed out of his comfy bed. How was he supposed to sleep with all that interesting racket going on outside—rain spitting against the windows and here and there someone switching on a light in the sky? It was enjoyable to watch, though as much as he liked to explore the big, exciting world beyond the door of his cottage, he didn't like getting wet.

He padded past his human, who was staring at that big screen on her desk, and crept into the hallway. He liked the night when most humans chose to do nothing but watch screens or snuggle up in their beds. It was the best time for hunting and discovery. He could find adventure even in his own cottage, but humans missed it all. Really, there was no understanding them.

Their feline houseguest was waiting in the hall, her fluffy tail curled around her. At least she wasn't wearing that ridiculous collar anymore. It was about time.

He twitched his whiskers and ambled past her into the kitchen, knowing she would follow. She knew enough not to waste the dark by sleeping it away. Together they checked out their bowls. His was empty, but a few morsels lingered in hers. He waited until she turned to snoop under the refrigerator door before lapping them up. Seniority had its privileges.

He ambled into the living room and leaped up onto the back of the couch. Yes! His human had not pulled the drapes over the big bay window yet. But she would before she went to bed.

The other cat settled beside him, swishing her tail in anticipation.

The raindrops tapped against the window and streamed downward. He used to try to catch them with his paw, but he had learned long ago that the exercise was futile.

He watched, ears perked, eyes peeled. When the light cracked across the *sky, it lit up the lawn and the woods beyond. But there were no squirrels or birds tonight. Likely they were hunkered down wherever squirrels and birds went in a storm. Still, he could never tell when something might pop up to challenge his kingdom. He could be patient.*

The other cat, growing bored, began swatting at the string beside the drapes.

He knew he must indulge her silly antics. After all, she was one of his kind. Besides, he had to admit he was getting used to her company.

She pawed at the string, lost her balance, and dropped down to the couch pillows with a startled meow.

Then he heard a sound. What was that? A raccoon braving the storm to forage around the door? A mouse or a bird pecking at some crumb a human might have left behind? He felt a tingle all the way to the stub of his tail. He crouched low on the back of the sofa, flattened his ears, and listened. He sniffed the air.

Something was different. This was a human smell. A human noise.

Light flashed through the sky again, though the rain had lessened, and that was when he saw them. Two humans. One was hiding in the bushes, and the other stood on the step to his cottage. He knew the one on the step. It was the human who dragged his new friend on a leash.

Now the human was knocking on the door.

He made a warning noise in his throat and hopped down with his friend close behind him. It was time to hide his houseguest.

He heard his person scrape her chair back from her desk as he scooted into the closet across from the front door. It was open just a crack, a crack that widened as his friend jumped in at the same time.

When his human left the closet open, he sometimes liked to explore its dark corners. It had a shelf at the very back, and he had hidden there before. Now, he would hide his friend. He'd hide her where the human with black hair and little round windows over her eyes couldn't find her.

The knocking grew louder.

He growled a warning to his friend to stay on the shelf and crept out of the closet to watch as his person went to the front door.

It had been one of those stormy nights that Faith usually found invigorating. Without the distractions of pleasant weather or the lure of shopping in Lighthouse Bay, she could concentrate on things that needed to be done at home.

Stormy nights could also make her reflective, so she would have to focus on keeping nostalgia and dreaminess at bay. Faith wondered what Wolfe was doing on this rainy night. She allowed herself to hope he might call or—even better—stop by the cottage to say hello. But then she sighed as she recalled his worry when he had come to the library earlier.

Faith wondered if Wolfe knew how important he was becoming to her—how something in her had awakened like a hidden spring, almost from the moment she'd met him. They were from different worlds, yet he seemed comfortable in hers, unless she was reading him wrong. Was there a place where their two worlds could come together?

The storm had surged in fits and starts throughout the evening, but now it had settled somewhat, leaving a steady rain.

She heard Watson and Faja scrambling around the house and smiled. Watson was a perennial night prowler—inside or out. It sounded like he had recruited a playmate to chase his catnip mouse or his favorite toy. The Ragdoll seemed even livelier since the collar had come off, and she appeared to enjoy leaping high in the air or scrambling after Watson. Faith knew her cat would miss Faja when the time came for her to go.

She picked up Faja's collar from her desk where she'd put it after removing it. The clunky thing was a menace. It had caught in the doorstop behind the kitchen door, nearly choking Faja in the process. Faith determined to replace it with something lighter and thinner as soon as she could.

The collar was heavy, not to mention ugly, with large plastic jewels glued onto the leather strap. She'd seen similar fake gems sold in bulk quantities at craft stores. There were six large gems about the size of a nickel and three more about the size of a penny. They weren't flat like coins but octagonal and raised. She twirled the collar around idly on her fingers and noticed that one of the large gems had loosened at its base.

Faith tucked the thin edge of her letter opener in the gap and watched the plastic bauble loosen even more and drop almost weightlessly onto her desk. Curious, she studied the darkened spot of leather where the gem had once been and noticed a faint crosshatching. It might have been caused by glue residue, but it seemed too perfect.

The next large gem—a gaudy green stone—was more resistant, but Faith pried at it with the letter opener until it, too, loosened and gave way. A similar crosshatching marked its spot. Intrigued, she picked at it, but the leather was too thick for her letter opener.

She ran to the kitchen for a paring knife. The collar would be no good now—with or without the gems—but she continued to cut away, first at the leather, then at a cloth lining beneath it.

Something sparkled as the knife slid through the lining. Faith gasped in astonishment as small, clear jewels spilled onto her desk.

In a flash, she knew what the jewels were. They were what someone had been searching for in Declan's suite and in his apartment. They might even be the reason he had been killed.

Her mind went immediately to the news story she'd been exploring earlier about the Boston jewelry heist and the unrecovered diamonds. Declan had been involved and had hidden the stash in plain sight—well, almost plain sight—around Faja's neck.

No wonder he'd watched Faja so carefully and kept her caged.

Now his extreme reaction to seeing his pet without a collar made sense.

The shock of the discovery coincided with a loud clap of thunder as rain fell with renewed vigor on the roof.

A series of claps. No, someone was knocking on her cottage door. She checked the clock on the wall—almost eight thirty and fully dark.

The knocking came again—louder—and in rhythm with the pounding of her heart.

Had she heard a car drive up? No one would be calling now. Unless it was Wolfe.

With a soaring heart and trembling fingers, Faith shoved the collar and the jewels into the desk drawer beneath the narrow shelf that held her keyboard. She hurried to the foyer.

Faith pushed aside the curtain. Edna stood on the doorstep, huddled under a red-and-blue striped umbrella. Faith groaned. She'd said the woman could come by to see Faja. But why, oh why, had she said to come anytime? She glanced back at her desk with its unbelievable contents and drew a deep, sustaining breath.

"I'm soaked to the skin," Edna said. "I had no idea the weather was so bad."

She did not, however, appear to have been gravely affected. Her shoes were wet, her raincoat streaked, but her hair retained its careful coiffure. She must have driven and left her car out back. What on earth would compel her to come outside in such awful weather?

Faith stared at her, no words of welcome coming to mind.

"I'm sorry to call so late, but I just wanted to see Faja. And you were kind enough to say I could stop by anytime." Tears or rain glistened on her cheeks. "Where is she?"

Faith turned and glanced around, surprised that Watson at least hadn't immediately appeared. "She's around here somewhere," she said soothingly, trying to recover her manners. "Please come inside. Let me take your coat. You must be chilled. April rains can go right through a person."

Edna entered the foyer but didn't remove her coat. "I don't want to disturb you. I'll only stay a moment."

"I have tea ready," Faith said, puzzled. "It'll warm you up." She ushered her into the living room and gestured to the sofa. "Won't you sit down?"

"Well, all right," Edna said, clearly uncomfortable. "But you needn't bother with tea."

Fine with me, Faith thought. She needed to get rid of Edna and deal with the discovery in her desk a few feet away. "Watson! Faja!" she called.

But there was no patter of feet, no answering meows.

Faith smiled reassuringly. "Maybe they're hiding because of the storm." But she knew Watson was seldom put off by storms. She looked toward the front door and noticed her cat sitting there. "Oh, there's Watson."

He remained near the door, his green eyes wide, ears erect. His watching pose, Faith recognized.

Edna turned to stare at the tuxedo cat with a noticeable scowl.

"Faja's around somewhere," Faith said, picking up the red jingle ball that Faja was partial to. She bounced it noisily across the floor.

Seconds later, the Ragdoll pushed her nose through a crack in the door of the hall closet. She raced past Watson and the couch where Edna sat and pawed at the ball, pushing it toward Faith.

Edna scooted forward to sit on the edge of the sofa.

"You can see she's just fine," Faith said. "She and Watson love exploring together."

"But where's her collar?" Edna asked. She knitted her eyebrows together. "If she gets lost, no one will know who she belongs to."

"I don't let her outside," Faith said, her mind beginning to whirl. "She's been safe inside the cottage since she arrived."

Declan had demanded to know where Faja's collar was that very first day. Was it possible that Edna also knew what was inside it? But that didn't make sense. She could have easily grabbed Faja right away after Declan's death, but she had made no move to take her. No one had. If someone had known what the cat was carrying, he or she would have tried to seize her. Or had the realization struck only later?

The ball Faja had been batting around disappeared under the couch.

As Faja scurried to retrieve it, pawing under the couch, Edna reached down and scooped the cat up. She stood abruptly, holding Faja fast in her arms. "That's all well and good, but she'll need her identifying tags. If you'll just get her collar for me, I'll be on my way." She twitched her nose and sniffed, her eyes already beginning to turn red.

"Excuse me?" Faith was aghast.

"I do thank you for your time, but you see, I'm taking Faja with me," Edna explained as though talking to a child. "I'm leaving tonight. I simply must return to my duties, and Faja is my responsibility." She stifled a sneeze.

"But you can't do that," Faith blurted in utter confusion. Edna was allergic to Faja, and it was no secret that she didn't have fond feelings for the cat. After Declan died, she had waited days to make sure the animal was okay. Why the sudden rush to take the cat that didn't even belong to her? "The retreat doesn't end until tomorrow, and Ms. Russell explained to you this afternoon—"

"I have no more time to waste," Edna interrupted, gripping Faja under one arm the way one might carry a sack of potatoes. She held out her free hand. "Give me the collar, and I'll get going."

Faith's pulse raced, and her mouth went as dry as desert dust. She remained rooted to the spot. "I'm afraid I can't do that," she said quietly. "It isn't Faja you want, is it? You know about the robbery. You know what your boss was hiding, don't you?"

Edna's eyes flashed as her face drained of color. Her mouth dropped open.

"You were at the Wellman Library near the site of that robbery six months ago," Faith stated. "You were in on it, and you've found out where Declan hid the jewels."

"I don't know what you're talking about," Edna said. "I only came here to retrieve Faja." Her lips began to tremble, and sweat broke out on her forehead.

"Is that why you killed him?" Faith took a step closer to the trembling woman.

"No! He betrayed me," Edna admitted. "He said we would be together. He said the money would help us make a fresh start in a new place, but he lied. All the time it was *her* he wanted." She sneezed.

While Edna was momentarily distracted, Faja scrambled out of her grasp and scampered into the kitchen.

"Declan said he loved me," Edna moaned. "He said he would prove it by giving me the jewels in that brown case. He said he was finally going to tell me where he'd hidden them. But it was a lie. They were fake! I threw them in the ocean after—"

"After you poisoned him," Faith finished for her. "Is that how you got rid of the bottle? In the ocean?"

Edna suddenly raised herself, squared her shoulders, and became eerily calm. "Of course," she said, as though they were discussing the weather. "Now, give me that collar. I need to go."

Faith shook her head. "It doesn't belong to you," she said simply. "It didn't belong to Declan either. You must do the right thing now. Tell the truth. It's not too late."

"It is too late," Edna said with a not-altogether-sane smile. "And too late for you. You don't think I came here alone, do you? He's right outside your door, and he's listening to every word."

Faith felt her heart sink. *Colin Kilpatrick*, she thought, *the third member of the burglary ring.*

18

The front door burst open, and a man stormed inside on a blast of wind.

At the same second, Watson shot out the door before Faith could stop him.

She gasped when she realized that the man was not Colin.

Eric McCandless whipped around as Watson sped past him. He stared after the cat for a second, stepped inside the cottage, and shut the door. Then he gave Faith a crooked smile that didn't reach his deep-set eyes. "Well, Miss Newberry, I see that my unwelcome presence has become necessary."

Faith stared in mute surprise. Her mind whirled as she put the pieces together. Eric McCandless, the mysterious figure at the stables, the man spying on Brooke, listening to conversations. Moving like the wind, ghostlike on those quick-stepping feet that now dripped water on her floor. He hadn't come to the retreat to absorb American literature but to claim a stolen treasure.

Eric removed a black ski cap and tossed it onto the floor. His hair lay matted and flat. "Edna has obviously been unable to bring you around to our way of thinking," he said in a mocking tone as he smoothed his mustache.

Faith remained silent.

"I can see you're surprised, but I thought a bright lady like you would have figured it out by now," Eric sneered. "You also should be smart enough to know how foolish it would be to continue to resist. Just get the mangy feline, and there will be no need for this." He opened his jacket, revealing a pistol tucked into the narrow waistband of his trousers.

Faith struggled to recapture the breath that had left her when Eric stormed inside. *Think, think!* She was alone, and no one had any idea what was going on. No one would guess that two desperate people had invaded her home. Were they desperate enough to kill her? She scolded herself for imagining the worst. She had to focus.

Then she remembered her cell phone in her pocket. But how could she possibly get a message off to Wolfe or to the police?

"I tried to make her understand," Edna said, sounding not quite sane and more like a child about to be punished.

Faja came padding into the living room. The cat glanced around with innocent blue eyes, then promptly sat down and began to groom herself. She would soon be looking for Watson, who had escaped out the front door in all the confusion.

"Ah, there's the little wonder herself," Eric said, taking a step toward Faja. "Good thing she didn't run out the door with her friend." He looked up sharply at Faith. "But she's not completely dressed, is she?"

"She took it off and wouldn't give it to me," Edna grumbled.

"Sit down," Eric commanded, pointing at the couch.

Edna complied, her lower lip protruding.

Eric turned to Faith. "We refer of course to the collar that was around her neck. Where is it?"

Faith forced herself to remain calm and not allow her gaze to roam in the direction of the computer desk where the collar and the jewels lay in the hidden drawer. She stared directly into Eric's eyes. "Do you really think I would keep a valuable item like that here in my house?"

Eric frowned, obviously taken aback.

Faith seized the moment. "We know about the robbery six months ago. We know that you and Edna and Declan stole those diamonds. The police will be coming for you very soon."

"For a smart lady, you're lousy at bluffing. They don't know squat, or they would have hauled that bumbling woman away." Eric jerked his thumb toward Edna, who sat sniffling on the couch.

Faja jumped up onto the back of the couch and paced from one end to the other, causing new fits of allergic woe for Edna.

"Why did you kill Declan?" Faith asked, trying to stall for time.

"She didn't have the brains to check the fake rocks he gave her before she doctored his dinner," Eric huffed. "We wouldn't have had to go through all this trouble to find the real ones if she'd used her head."

"It wasn't supposed to kill him!" Edna cried out through fresh tears. "You said it would only make him sick, keep him quiet until things settled down and we got our share of the diamonds." She rubbed her red-rimmed eyes. "I didn't want to kill him. I loved him!"

Faith shuddered. Declan had no idea what kind of friends he'd been partnering with.

"Loved him?" Eric scoffed. "He's the jerk who did the double-dealing. We agreed that he would hide the stuff until things cooled down. But then the fool said it was a mistake, and he wanted to give the diamonds back."

"I wouldn't have even cared about the jewels, but he betrayed me!" Edna wailed.

Eric glared at Edna, his eyes glittering. "You might forget about it and give up a fortune. But not me. I figured out where the stash was. It was all in that letter."

Eric had been hiding behind the Peter Pan fountain. He'd heard Laura tell Brooke about the letter Declan had written to Colin. The letter of remorse in which he spoke of passing on a curse—the curse of striving for riches.

The lines written first by Mark Twain flashed through her memory: *"It is good to begin life poor; it is good to begin life rich—these are wholesome; but to begin it prospectively rich! The man who has not experienced it cannot imagine the curse of it."*

Faith had pondered what Declan had meant by passing on a curse that could also be a blessing. *Still, it is a curse I pass on—or a blessing, if carefully considered.* Had Declan been trying to turn the jewels over to his brother in the hope that he would give them back to their rightful owner?

"The letter was so poetic, wasn't it?" Eric went on sarcastically. He was clearly enjoying his power over Edna. "'A man who carries a cat by the tail learns something he can learn in no other way.' The cat was the clue, and I finally got it. Declan was a clever fox but not clever enough. I knew the secret hiding place had to be in that fancy collar his cat wore."

Faith's cell phone jangled noisily in her pocket. She reached to pull it out.

"Don't!" Eric shouted, whirling around. Then in a more controlled tone, he said, "Don't do that."

"But it's my boyfriend's ring," Faith said, making up a story in order to answer the phone. "He always calls at this time in the evening. If I don't answer, he'll know something's wrong. He's at the manor, and he'll come running over here in a flash."

Eric glared at her, his eyes protruding wildly from their deep sockets. The muscles in his jaw began to throb as he hesitated. "All right, answer it. But if you say anything out of the ordinary, you'll be very sorry. Trust me." He rested his right hand on the pistol tucked in his waistband.

Faith checked the screen and saw that it was Wolfe. She put the phone to her ear. In the panicky few seconds when she considered how she might tip off Wolfe that something was wrong, her father's first name came to her. "Hello, Martin," she said brightly.

"What?" Wolfe asked.

"Yes, I'm fine. Are you okay, Martin?" Faith said cheerfully. *Please let me sound normal at least to Eric.*

"Is something wrong?" Wolfe asked.

She giggled. "Oh, you say the sweetest things."

"Something is wrong," Wolfe said, anxiety in his voice. "What's going on?"

Faith forced herself to appear nonchalant. "Listen, Martin, I have cookies in the oven. If you keep saying things like that, they'll burn to a crisp."

"Watson is here, and he's acting very strangely. He—"

"Tomorrow night?" Faith interrupted. "I'd love to, but let me call you in the morning. I have to go." She clicked off and stuffed the phone back into her pocket with trembling fingers. She felt her heart pound with hope. Wolfe could run to her cottage in five minutes. Maybe even less.

"Enough fooling around. Where is the collar?" Eric scanned the living room, as though he would spy it cast off in some corner.

"I told you I'd be a fool to keep something so valuable here," Faith insisted. "The smart thing would be to keep it in the safe at the manor."

"If you had turned it in, the police would be crawling around all over this place. Instead, it's quiet as a tomb." Eric fixed her with a threatening stare. "I hate lies."

He's deep into robbery and murder, but he hates lies? Faith mused. And as a matter of fact, she hadn't lied, except by omission. Strange how these thoughts occurred to her in a situation that was clearly dangerous and growing more so as the moments ticked by. But she was angry too. Greed had terrible consequences, leading to a man's death.

"You can't possibly hope to get away with this," Faith said evenly.

Edna sniffled as she tried to swat Faja off the back of the couch.

Eric turned to Edna. "Get up! Start searching this place right now." He kept one hand on his gun, and he used the other hand to pull out the drawer of a nearby end table and dump its contents onto the floor. "Check the bedroom."

Edna jumped up and fled from the living room.

Eric tossed couch pillows, then swiped the mantel surface and bookshelves while keeping Faith in his sight. It would be a matter of minutes—or even seconds—before he got to her computer desk.

Faith could only hope and pray that Wolfe would act in time. She knew he had understood that she was in trouble.

A clatter and a shout came from the rear of the cottage.

Eric pulled the gun from his belt and waved it at Faith, jerking his head to indicate she was to precede him to the source of the sound.

Faja, who had scampered after Edna, crouched on top of the bed, staring down at the woman sprawled on the floor, her leg twisted at an odd angle.

"That atrocious animal tripped me," Edna complained. "I can't get up."

The rug at the base of Faith's bed lay askew, turned inside out at one end. Faith had recently purchased it for her newly polished wood floor and had neglected to buy the rubberized rug pad that would keep it from slipping. Now, she realized, that omission might just buy the time needed for help to come.

Eric cursed at Edna.

Edna ignored him as she writhed on the floor and cried out in pain.

"She's hurt," Faith said, kneeling beside Edna.

"Leave her," Eric ordered, his voice as chilling as the cold steel of the gun pressed against her shoulder. "No more time for games. I want the collar now."

Despite the terror of the moment, Faith was sure she heard the rumble of tires approaching the cottage. Sirens, if they came, would spook her captor, and he might use the gun he aimed at her. She stood and turned around with a calm she couldn't have explained. "You can't do this," she said. "You know it's wrong. Just stop now before anything worse happens."

Edna wailed as she struggled to get up.

"I think her leg is broken, and she's hit her head too," Faith said. She pulled out her cell phone. "We have to call for help."

Eric snatched the phone from her hand and whipped it across the room. "I'm at the end of my patience with you." He waved the gun shakily, and Faith could see that he was sweating. "You're coming with me. We're getting out of here," he said through clenched teeth.

Did he now believe that the collar was in the safe at the manor? Did he plan to force her to retrieve it under the cover of night?

"We're going out the back way," he spat. "Move!"

His vehicle or Edna's must be behind her cottage.

What was she going to do if Eric commanded her to open the safe at the manor? Faith had no way to open it even if the jewels had been there. Which of course they were not.

She headed for the kitchen, her heart pounding. Eric was on her heels. Faja padded after them and leaped up onto the refrigerator while Faith fumbled with the lock. It had been sticking, and it was difficult to open with the advent of warm, wet weather. Now with her fingers trembling, it resisted her attempts to turn the knob.

"Open it!" Eric shouted.

"I can't," Faith said. "It's stuck."

Eric shoved the gun into his belt and tugged at the door with both hands. Suddenly he let out a roar as Faja pounced onto his head in a streak of white-and-brown fury.

Watson had attacked a trespasser from his perch on the refrigerator before, but Faith never imagined the docile Ragdoll had it in her.

Eric spun around, searching for the cat, but Faja fled, leaving her victim dazed and cursing.

At the same moment, the front door burst open. Amid a cacophony of voices, Wolfe rushed in and pinned Eric to the wall.

Behind Wolfe, Officers Bryan Laddy and Mick Tobin descended. They swiftly restrained Eric and slapped handcuffs on him.

Faith collapsed against the door, then felt familiar arms wrap around her—arms that never felt so amazing.

"I'm so relieved you're all right," Wolfe whispered.

19

"I couldn't believe it when I heard," Eileen said, passing a tray of crepes and sausages to Faith. "Who would have guessed that Declan had hidden diamonds in his cat's collar?"

"Our clever Faith guessed," Midge said. "It makes me smile to picture that sweet little Faja tripping up his two accomplices." She raised her glass of orange juice to her fuchsia lips.

The retreat had ended, and most of the guests had already checked out. Now Faith, Eileen, Brooke, Midge, Wolfe, and Marlene—along with Watson—were enjoying a Sunday brunch in the manor's dining room. It had been Wolfe's idea, but Marlene had made the arrangements and instructed Brooke that she wasn't to lift a finger.

"It's been quite a week," Marlene said, sweeping a hand across her forehead in a show of relief. "But we can all be grateful that it's over."

Faith smiled as she glanced around the table at her friends. It had indeed been a suspenseful week, ending with the frightening events of the previous evening. She had shared the story with her friends, including how the police had been closing in on Eric and hadn't been far away when Wolfe alerted them that something was amiss at Faith's cottage.

As for Faja, the Ragdoll had probably been weaving around Edna's feet and tripped her accidentally. But it had been enough to disable her and buy Faith some time for Wolfe to arrive. So, in a way, she supposed the Ragdoll did have her revenge for being treated as a mule, not to mention being kept in a cage and dragged on a leash.

Watson had done his part, too, by running off to find Wolfe and attempting to alert him that something was wrong at the cottage.

Watson was curled up in her lap after enjoying a treat of sausage-mixed kibble. She stroked his head and his silken back.

No doubt he would miss Faja. The cat would be going home with Colin to his Boston apartment. But Faith suspected that Colin would be coming this way from time to time to see Laura. Chances were good he'd bring Faja along for a visit. What a relief it was that the young man training to be a veterinary technologist was the honorable person he had seemed to be.

"Declan wanted to give the diamonds back," Faith said wistfully.

"So what happened?" Brooke asked.

"Eric wasn't about to lose his share of the money he'd get for them," Faith explained. "He made Edna find out where Declan hid them. Once she thought he had finally given them to her, she slipped the Ziophaine into his dinner, thinking it would only incapacitate him long enough for her and Eric to get away. But the gems Declan gave her were fake."

"How did Eric figure out where the real diamonds were?" Midge asked.

"It must have been when he overheard my conversation with Laura at the Peter Pan fountain," Brooke guessed. "We were discussing the letter Declan sent to his brother."

Faith nodded.

"Where did they get the drug?" Eileen asked.

"The chief told me that Eric got it through his connections in the black market," Wolfe said. "Edna threw away the evidence, but the police won't have any trouble making the charges against them stick. They've dug up quite a dossier on Eric McCandless."

Brooke shook her head. "Poor Declan," she murmured. "He had so much potential. I wish . . ."

They all fell silent for a moment, knowing what Brooke was probably wishing.

Then Wolfe said, "The good news is that the jewels will be returned to their rightful owner, and our guests here at the manor have been protected."

"I doubt that we'll see Professor George again," Marlene said with an ironic grin. "It's never pleasant to be reminded of sins of the past."

"Did Clement really plagiarize someone else's work?" Eileen asked.

"He insists he didn't, but apparently he did borrow a little too freely from another expert's work," Marlene answered. "Enough that it cost him his job. It's unlikely he'll make that mistake again."

His job and more, Faith thought sadly. She regretted that the breach between Declan and Clement had not been healed, and she wished the best for Clement in future days.

"But Corinna and Madeline say they're coming back again soon," Marlene continued. "They were most complimentary and wanted to especially thank you, Faith." She frowned as she caught her eye. "They didn't say what for."

A warm glow of satisfaction settled over Faith as she thought of the Morrissey sisters. Madeline's secret had been kept from disclosure, and hopefully her position at the university had been safeguarded. Corinna had made an appointment to get her sister back into therapy.

"Here's to the ladies of the Candle House Book Club." Wolfe raised his coffee cup in a toast. "Without you and the good officers of Lighthouse Bay's finest, the mystery might never have been solved."

"Hear! Hear!" Eileen said, leaning over to kiss her niece on the cheek. She winked at Wolfe. "Thank goodness you phoned Faith at precisely the right moment."

"When she called me by her father's name, I knew something was up," Wolfe said. He turned to Faith, shaking his head. "It took ten years off my life."

"I'm just glad it's finally over," Brooke said in a small voice. Her eyes were misty with tears, but her face radiated happiness. "I don't know how to thank all of you for believing in me and supporting me through this ordeal."

"Never was any question. All for one and one for all," Eileen said as she pushed back from the table. She stood and picked up her shoulder bag. "But I have to fly." She gave them a sweeping farewell wave. "Cheers, everyone!"

"I need to get going too," Midge said, rising.

Brooke and Marlene likewise departed.

When only Faith, Wolfe, and Watson were left at the table, a satisfying stillness settled. A soft breeze drifted in from the window, bringing the scent of cherry blossoms.

Wolfe's hand closed over hers.

She turned to drink in his smile and the tender warmth in his eyes. Something of urgency lay in their blue depths. It appeared that he wanted to say something but seemed at a loss to find the words.

"I've been thinking," Wolfe began, lightly squeezing her hand. "I would like to get to know you better. But I can't help but wonder if it would be appropriate to pursue a relationship since we work together."

Faith felt her heart flop around in her chest, as though it had forgotten its rhythm. It was what she'd hoped for, what she wanted, but she shared his concern. Was it really a good idea to pursue a romantic relationship with her boss? It would certainly make things awkward at the manor.

She swallowed, savoring the moment, the lovely idea that Wolfe truly cared about her as she did him. "I would like to get to know you better too, but I'm wondering the same thing."

"Well, I suggest we take it slowly," Wolfe said. "It sounds archaic, but may I have permission to court you?"

Faith smiled, feeling the warmth flow through her. "I'm open to that idea, sir," she said teasingly and yet affirming in the depths of her heart its splendid possibility.

Watson purred loudly.

"It seems as though Watson approves." He smiled and squeezed her hand before letting it go and rising from his chair. "And now, in appreciation of a job well done, Miss Castleton Librarian, I hereby give you tomorrow off. On one condition."

"And what would that be?" Faith asked.

"You spend it with me."

.

Victorian Mansion
Flower Shop Mysteries™

S et on sparkling Puget Sound in the cozy
island town of Turtle Cove, Washington,
the stories in this enthralling series are
good old-fashioned whodunits chock-full of
fascinating family secrets, breathtaking scenery,
heartwarming discoveries, and the unbreakable
bonds of female friendships.

If you love the great outdoors, gardens, birds,
flowers, and a good mystery book ... then you'll
love Annie's *Victorian Mansion Flower Shop Mysteries!*

AnniesFiction.com

YOUR FEEDBACK MEANS A LOT TO US!

Up to this point, we've been doing all the writing. Now it's *your* turn!

Tell us what you think about this book, the characters, the bad guy, or anything else you'd like to share with us about this series. We can't wait to hear from *you*!

Log on to give us your feedback at:
https://www.surveymonkey.com/r/CastletonLibrary

Annie's FICTION